Pearls Gone Wild

Book 6 in the Samantha Kidd Mystery Series

Diane Vallere

Polyester Press
www.polyesterpress.com

PEARLS GONE WILD
Book 6 in the Samantha Kidd Mystery Series
A Polyester Press Mystery

Print ISBN: 9781939197283

Printed in the United States of America.

Dedication

To Coco

Also by Diane Vallere

Samantha Kidd Mysteries
Designer Dirty Laundry
Buyer, Beware
The Brim Reaper
Some Like It Haute
Grand Theft Retro
Pearls Gone Wild

Madison Night Mad for Mod Mysteries
"Midnight Ice" Prequel Novella
Other People's Baggage
Pillow Stalk
That Touch of Ink
With Vics You Get Eggroll
The Decorator Who Knew Too Much (April 2017)

Material Witness Mysteries
Suede to Rest
Crushed Velvet
Silk Stalkings

Costume Shop Mystery Series
A Disguise To Die For
Masking for Trouble
Dressed to Confess (Aug 2017)

1

"Men are rats!" Cat said. She threw a dinner plate into her kitchen sink and it shattered on contact.

"They're not all rats," I said.

"Name one who's not a rat. Go ahead, name one." Before I had a chance to answer, she continued. "My husband is a rat. His bosses are rats." She grabbed another plate. "My brother is kind of a rat, don't you think?"

"Cat, I don't think it's my place to say whether or not your brother is a rat."

"He's a rat, trust me. You don't know because you chose Nick instead of him." She brought the dish down against the sink. It bounced off, unbroken. She looked at it, confused, and then turned it over and looked at the bottom. "Corelle. Well, that's not satisfying at all." She tossed it onto the counter where it skidded until hitting a loaf of bread.

Cat Lestes was a local boutique owner, a friend, and one of those people who make you constantly feel rumpled if only because she's always immaculately dressed. I'd never seen so much as a hair of her striking red, asymmetrical haircut out of place...until tonight. Her husband spent more than half of his life on the road and, as if that hadn't been enough space, he'd told her earlier this evening that he needed a break. It turned out his definition of "break" differed from hers; he was moving out. Considering Cat was eight months pregnant, George's timing seemed suspicious.

"I'm pretty sure George is just going through a phase, like last month when you said you wanted to run away and join a convent."

She picked up a mug and shook it at me. "Nuns don't have to deal with swollen ankles," she said.

I stepped forward and put my hands on her wrists. "He didn't cheat on you, he didn't ask for a divorce. He's just asked for some space. He probably was thinking about the baby and about how his life is going to change."

She glared at me for a moment, and then deflated like a balloon twenty-four hours after a twelve-year-old's birthday party. Her normally size two frame shrunk, causing her pregnant belly to protrude. It looked like a tiny nerf basketball had been strapped to her waist under her chocolate brown knit dress.

"There are times to think about making more money and there are times to be there for your wife," she said. "He should have known that."

I pried the mug—the next about-to-be-broken item in her arsenal—from her grip and set it on the counter and then wrapped her in a hug. Cat was like me in the fact that she wasn't particularly touchy-feely, but at the moment it seemed like we both needed it.

When we pulled apart, I pointed to the living room. "You go sit down. I'll clean up in here."

"It's my mess," she argued.

"Let me do this for you."

She nodded and left me alone with the broken dishes. Cat lived in a split level house in a residential neighborhood in Wyomissing. Her neighbors were in the post-retirement, 65+ range and were friendly but not nosy. I often thought of myself as a woman who lived alone in a house probably too big for her, but even before Cat's marital troubles, she'd been in a similar boat because of her husband's travel. Except now she was on her own with a full time job and a baby on the way. I couldn't begin to imagine the pressures she felt.

As I collected pieces of broken dishes and glass from the floor, I heard what sounded like the local news coming from her TV. These days it was mostly stories about the weather or the occasional car theft from one of the local malls. Thus represented the city of Ribbon, Pennsylvania, where we split our time (and our residents) between do-gooders and criminals. At least that's how it seemed since I moved back two years ago. And here I'd thought trading New York City for small town life would lead to a more peaceful existence.

Cat's proclamation that all men were rats landed on deaf ears thanks to my relationship with Nick Taylor. While her husband had let her down at a time when he should have been there for her, my love life was chugging along, hitting all the right notes.

Nick was a local shoe designer who kept an apartment in Italy, and shortly after my birthday in May, he'd left to meet with the factories about his upcoming collection. Our relationship was not without problems—many of which explained why we'd broken up once since making the shift from business colleagues (nine years) to on-again/off-again couple (two years)—but ever since I'd saved his father's life,

Nick seemed willing to overlook the problems (inconveniences?) that came with dating me. And I understood the needs of his business and the fact that spending six months out of each year in Europe was part of his life. But I'd be lying if I said I wasn't looking forward to Nick coming home for the holidays.

I swept the broken pieces of china into the dustpan and then into the trash. Cat's kitchen—her whole house, really—was usually immaculate. I did a double take when I saw the two errant grape tomatoes and scattering of green peas that I swept up with the broken china. Maybe her housekeeping skills were relaxing, but at least she was still keeping up with her daily vegetable intake. That put her one step ahead of me.

"Stupid bastard!" Cat yelled from the living room. Moments later, there was a thud.

I dropped the dustpan and broom into the sink and ran to the living room. Cat was on the floor with her feet splayed out in front of her. Her dress was hiked up to her hips and between her knees was a partially empty bowl. Across the room, popcorn was scattered around the base of the TV.

"What's wrong? What happened?"

She pointed to the screen. "The news is doing a profile on the rat. 'Local businessmen do good.' That's a joke. He didn't do any good by leaving me. Just because he's helping his company hand out free ornaments tonight that doesn't make him a saint. It's Christmas. Where are the stories about stolen cars and thefts at the mall? Where are all the shady Santas?"

I leaned forward and plunked the remote from her hand. "Are you okay?"

"Retail. Holidays. Pregnant. Rat husband. Keep up, Sam. I thought I could rely on the news to match my mood, but no. It's like they got tired of reporting on all of the retail theft so they're looking for feel-good stories. The rest of the year it's all politics, hate crimes, and misdemeanors, but when I need it?

'Local businessmen do good.' And these people call themselves reporters."

I sat down next to her. "Where are they—your mall?" Cat's boutique, Catnip, was in the Ribbon Designer Outlet Mall. "Is it a special shopping night? Are there discounts?"

"It's the lighting of the mall Christmas tree. Kenner & Winn are the hosts—that's the company George works for. If George was a good guy, he'd be here, not at a party handing out baubles. The news should focus on the stores, not the vendors. We're the ones who make it through the battleground of December shopping so people can have presents under the tree. But we're like the elves. Totally under appreciated." She threw another fistful of popcorn at the TV.

I bent down and corralled the spilled popcorn into a pile, and then, using both hands, transferred it onto a *Glamour* magazine that Cat had left open to the "Fashion Don'ts" section. I left the magazine on the coffee table and spun around so I could face her.

"I know this is going to sound strange coming from me, but I think you need to calm down." She stared at me but didn't say a word. "I know you're mad at George, and I understand why. But you can't let that anger spill out onto everything else. Didn't the doctor warn you about your blood pressure?"

"Yes, but it's not like I can sit around and relax. Not now. There's going to be another mouth to feed and I don't trust that rat to do the right thing. Employee turnover is at an all-time high. I tried to hire extra staff to take some of the pressure off me, but as soon as I train one person, another one quits. Yesterday one of my associates resigned at the end of her shift. She got an invite to go skiing for the holidays and is leaving tomorrow. I didn't even get two weeks' notice. Honestly, what is wrong with people? I told her I was surprised she even bothered to show up and you know what she said? She wanted to make sure she got her last paycheck."

"That's not very professional. I hope she doesn't want a referral."

"People don't think of retail jobs as professions. It's what they do while they figure out how to do what they want to do. It's frustrating."

"You need to cut yourself a break. My vacation just started. I'll help out whenever I can, but now is not the time to try to be superwoman."

My work history post-moving back to Ribbon had been spotty (at best). Earlier in the year I'd been gainfully employed at *Retrofit*, a start-up ezine that showcased current fashion trends and how they correlated to fashion history. My boss's big dreams of expansion had had disastrous results, and *Retrofit* was on its way to becoming yet another casualty on my resume, until an unlikely savior stepped in: Tradava.

Tradava was a mid-range retailer that actively pursued their share of the entry-level trend market. Their partnerships with design competitions and museum exhibits had kept their name in the news and their affiliation with mid-range fashion present. Their desire to produce a glossy magalog—a cross between a catalog and a magazine—led to a bit of creative thinking, and some smart person at the top of the food chain made the decision to buy *Retrofit* and bring us into the advertising fold.

Which meant I still had a job. Not just any job, either. One with health benefits and a 401K of my own. In the three months after my probationary period ended, I'd had a full blood workup, a physical, and an assortment of exams that covered the parts of me that needed to stay in working order. If medical came with a customer punch card like the sandwich shop, I'd be due for a freebie any day now.

I picked up the remote and cued up the guide. "Let's find something else to watch to distract you. Look—*Dial M for Murder* is on. Are you feeling Hitchcocky? Or maybe we need a Rom Com."

"I think you're right," she said. She put her palms on the sofa behind her and slowly lifted herself off the floor and onto the cushion. She smoothed her red hair with her hands and then stood up. "A distraction is a good idea." She crossed the room and picked up her handbag, and then pulled out a laminated card and waved it at me. "You feel like a party?"

"You didn't say anything about a party when you invited me over."

"That's because when I invited you over I didn't know we were going."

"Where are we going?"

"There. To the party. I should be there, not him. I'm the one who buys their product and sells it in my store. I want him to look me in the eye in a public place and let everybody know what he did."

"But I thought you said Kenner & Winn were jerks?"

"They are. And tonight they're the jerks who get to be the target to all of this misplaced anger."

I didn't get up. "Five minutes ago you were breaking china. Maybe you need to sit still for a couple of minutes—"

"If everything had gone according to plan, I was going to be in the middle of a romantic dinner tonight. But I'm not. That doesn't mean I have to sit here like a big fat blob. I can have a life too, right?"

I looked down at my outfit. Navy sweater and blue camo pants. At least my boots had heels. "I'm not dressed for a party."

"You look fine," she said, providing further evidence that she wasn't exactly herself. Under normal circumstances, Cat had particularly choice things to say about my occasional desire to shop the Army-Navy store (because blue camo is totally fabulous even if a non-hormonal Cat wouldn't agree).

"I really think it would be better if we stayed in." I pulled my phone out of my handbag. "Pick out a movie while I call Nick. I'll make you a fresh bowl of popcorn when I'm done."

I slipped from the living room into her den. "Hey, Kidd," he answered.

"Hey, Taylor."

"How's your Friday night?"

"Touch and go. I'm at Cat's. She's...her husband...things aren't really great right now. I'm acting as a calming force."

He laughed. "You're about as calming as a bed full of itching powder."

"I resent that!"

"Just saying you're not known for your ability to relax."

"I can relax just fine," I said. "What about you? Packing? Your flight takes off in a couple of hours, right?"

"Change of plans," he said. "There's a problem at one of the factories and I can't leave yet."

"You're not flying home tonight?" My positive outlook waivered. I wanted to feel all the things you feel at the beginning of a relationship, but I couldn't help wonder if, ten years down the line, Nick would be restless just like Cat's husband. "Is it a big problem?

"If I want to stay on production schedule with my new collection it would be best to fix it in person."

"Have you told your dad?"

This past May, Nick's life had been flipped on its head when his dad, recovering from a broken hip, moved in with him. In addition to the newly negotiated domestic situation, it had brought Nick and I closer. I'd learned a multitude of quirks about him that raised eyebrows. He learned the truth about my daily caloric intake. And yet, we were still together.

"Tonight's his poker night. It violates the rules of their game to use cell phones."

"Sounds like you're going to come home to cheap beer and stale chips."

"You fixed the chip situation with the golden Chip Clip you gave him the last time you were over. It's his favorite thing in the house."

"See? There is no limit to the problems I solve."

"Kidd, there's something I have to tell you. I told a friend to crash here while I was gone, but now that I have to stay, well, I didn't expect to have a roommate."

"Two bachelors in Italy. Should I be worried about you cruising for Italian women?"

"Kidd, she's not a bachelor. She's—the friend—is Amanda Ries."

If I'd been standing in Cat's kitchen, I might have picked up that unbreakable piece of Corelle, thrown it onto the floor, and then stomped on it a few times. Instead, I stood up and punched the hunter green leather chair behind the desk.

"Kidd, you know she's just a friend."

That wasn't the point, and I knew it, and I was pretty sure he knew it too. "I think I hear Cat calling me from the living room. I have to go." I hung up before he had a chance to reply.

When I returned to the living room, Cat was sprawled out on the sofa. The screen saver for *The First Wives Club* was on the TV. The remote control dangled from her hand. I took it and clicked off the TV.

"Get your handbag. We're going out."

"What changed your mind?"

"Turns out you were right. All men *are* rats."

2

FRIDAY NIGHT, 6:17 P.M.

Nick and Amanda were college friends who both worked as designers, though in different aspects of the industry. Their friendship, shared experience, and education had created a bond and she was a part of his life. The rational part of my brain knew there was nothing going on between them and not just because he'd told me. But my irrational side taunted me with all kinds of images: Nick and Amanda together on a seven hour flight. Nick and Amanda sharing a walk around Italy under a starry sky. And possibly the worst: Nick and Amanda sharing a margarita pizza. (I'm especially territorial when it comes to food.)

I'd had a spotty employment record after leaving my nine-year career as a designer shoe buyer for Bentley's New York and moving to Ribbon, Pennsylvania, and in that time I'd taken on whatever fashion-related work I could find. During Nick and my off-again period, I'd helped Amanda mount her first fashion show. I'd committed to the project before Nick and I had broken up, and it had been important for me to honor my commitment. Things hadn't gone exactly as planned. Nick's friendship with Amanda was something I'd have to learn to accept, just like Nick had to acknowledge my own friendship with Cat's brother, Dante. But either time one of their names came up, the reaction was the same: jealousy. And if we didn't find a way to deal with that, any relationship we had would be doomed.

I pushed thoughts of Nick and Amanda in Italy (with or without food) from my mind and drove Cat to the designer outlets. "Tell me about this party."

"Tom Kenner and Don Winn are the partners who own Kenner & Winn. They're jewelry wholesalers. They're co-sponsoring a shopping night at the mall to promote their jewelry line. George joined their company a couple of months ago and took over their biggest territory."

"Kenner & Winn. How come I never heard of them? I was a buyer for nine years before I moved here."

"Their specialty is licensee deals. Designers sign on with them to source products, but most designers don't want you to know where they get their products from because you could just cut out the middle man and get the merchandise without the name attached."

The nine years that I'd spent as a buyer had been in ladies designer shoes. Cat was right. I didn't buy directly from the factories, I bought from the designers. I could tell you a lot about how the shoe business worked, but the technical side was still something of a mystery to me.

"I never thought about it before but jewelry must be a high margin business."

"It is. There's no way to put a designer name on an item except on the packaging. You're getting double the mark-up for a designer name and only the people who follow high fashion know whether your jewelry is Chanel or Saint Laurent or Oscar."

"So this party is being sponsored by the men who import the product, right?"

"Yes, but don't worry, they're not fashion people. These guys are the ones with the money. They don't care about taste, they care about the bottom line. If I told them I wanted to start selling rhinestone-encrusted bras they'd find a way to supply them."

"So you've bought from them? For Catnip?"

She shook her head. "Only recently. I don't carry precious jewelry, and even if I had, I always thought it was a bad idea for George and me to mix our work life with our home life. Shows what I know. If I'd been one of his clients, I might have known he was on the verge of a mid-life crisis."

"But recently, you placed orders from Kenner & Winn?"

"Yes. One of his accounts canceled an order of pearls because Kenner & Winn missed the delivery window. I've been working on a luxury strategy for Catnip and George talked me into buying the canceled order."

"How's it selling?"

"It never had a chance to sell. It was stolen in a smash and grab. Merry Christmas to me," she said in a flat voice.

For those not in the know, a smash and grab is an in-and-out retail theft. The idea is that, if you're quick, you can break into a store, smash a glass case full of merchandise, grab as much as you can carry, and get out in less than a minute. Judging from where the security officers might be, even if they know a theft is taking place, you can be gone before they can catch up with you.

It's a bold way to steal. Most people get caught because they're either not fast enough or they get greedy and stay in the store too long. Sometimes thieves smash the first case they find and take armloads of items that have low resell value.

That's one of the ways you can tell if thieves know what they were doing.

"Was anything caught on camera?"

"The camera is mounted to the opposite side of the mall by the main entrance. The alarm went off, but by the time the police showed up, the merchandise was long gone."

"They got everything?"

She nodded. "Black Tahitian pearl necklaces. You remember them, right? The only one they didn't steal was the one you asked me to put on hold."

I'd seen the necklace in question last week during a quick shopping trip. As much as I'd wanted to splurge on it, the comma in the price had been a good deterrent from adding it to my list of must-haves. It sounded to me that the thieves knew what they were doing.

We arrived at the Ribbon Designer Outlets and I pulled up next to a twenty-something in a red jacket and black pants, exited the car, and headed toward a giant green tree. It was decorated in lustrous round ornaments that looked like oversized pearls and sparkling plastic gemstones. Thick ribbon printed with the Kenner & Winn logo had been loosely draped around the tree. Subtlety apparently wasn't high on the duo's agenda. White twinkle lights wound through the branches, and two spotlights on the ground were aimed at the top just in case you somehow missed the monstrosity.

I followed Cat to the entrance. A woman in a soft, chiffon duster, coordinating satin tank top, and palazzo pants stood next to a man in a tuxedo. Her lashes were so long I felt a breeze when she blinked. The man held out a hand to Cat. She shook it aggressively, though I didn't think she had much of a choice.

"Welcome to the Kenner & Winn holiday party. I'm Tom Kenner. This is my wife, Joyce."

"Cat Lestes," Cat said.

Tom turned toward the woman next to him. She looked at her husband first, and then at Cat. Her smile seemed disingenuous, although whether it was Cat and my presence or the fact that she was bored by the event that caused the reaction, I didn't know.

"Cat. Is that short for Catherine?" Joyce asked.

"Yes," Cat said.

"And you are?" Joyce said to me.

Before I could answer, Cat spoke up again. "This is Samantha. She's my partner."

"She means—" I started, but Cat put her hand on my arm. Tom and Joyce looked Cat's pregnant belly.

"Nice to see your kind taking such good care of each other," Tom said. He put his hand on Cat's belly and I felt her tense next to me. "Little one is going to be lucky, having two moms."

"Is Mr. Winn here?" Cat asked.

"Nope. We heard about some trouble with the exporter and he lost the coin toss. He'll be spending his holiday in India." He chuckled.

Joyce looked past me and gestured toward a cluster of people more appropriately dressed than I was. She extended a braceleted arm with long, well-manicured nails and directed us toward a waiter handing out pre-poured flutes of pink champagne just inside the store entrance. Behind them, a woman in an ivory pantsuit worked a coat check booth. It wasn't until after we were inside the store that I pinched Cat's arm.

"Ow! What was that for?"

"Partner?"

"Business partner. Why else would I bring you here tonight?"

"Friend, associate, customer..." I ticked off possible answers. "How come he doesn't know you're George's wife?" I asked. "Shouldn't he recognize you?"

"I've never met Tom or Joyce before. We haven't been to any company events for Kenner & Winn yet."

"Look on the bright side. He'll probably give you a set of hers and hers matching towels when you have the baby."

"They don't know I'm married to the rat." She looked over my shoulder and then scanned the rest of the room. "You don't see him, do you?"

"He's going to be here?" I asked. I dropped my voice to a whisper. "You're not going to cause a scene, are you?"

"Of course not. I'm a lady." She smoothed out her hair. "Go to the bar. You'll fit in more if you're holding a glass of champagne."

"I'd fit in more if you would have given me five minutes to change."

"I'm going to see what kind of non-alcoholic beverages they have." She pulled her long silk scarf from around her shoulders. "You're creative. Do something with this."

I weaved through the crowd in search of a private spot where I could work a makeover miracle on my G.I. Jane outfit. Pearlescent balloons had been blown up and scattered around the floor and hung from the ceiling. The coat check woman pointed to a public restroom and I went inside to change.

I pulled my sweater over my head, and then tied two ends of Cat's scarf around my neck. I tied the other two ends behind my back, creating a drape-front, open back top. My bra was an eyesore, so I took it off, which created a whole other set of problems. I found a roll of fabric tape in the bottom of my handbag and used it to, shall we say, secure my assets with a trick I'd learned from a stylist. I re-knotted the scarf and jumped up and down a few times to make sure everything was going to stay in place. The door to the bathroom opened. I flushed the toilet (cover story) and waited until feet appeared in the stall next to me before I left mine.

My sweater and bra were too cumbersome to fit in my handbag. I looked around for a place to stash them for later retrieval, but frankly, there was something a little skeevy about stashing clothes in a public restroom. I slid the window open and pushed the two items outside. They landed on a patch of brown grass behind a bare bush.

I washed my hands and ran my fingers through my hair. The other stall opened and a ghostly pale woman with full red lips and heavily arched eyebrows came out. Her jet black hair was slicked away from her face and a hibiscus was tucked behind one ear. She wore a skin tight yellow strapless dress that was cinched with a red patent leather belt. After washing and drying her hands, she pulled a tube of lipstick out of her handbag and touched up her pout.

A small bundle wrapped in tissue paper fell out of her bag and landed on the floor by her red patent leather peep toe pumps. I bent down and picked it up. "You dropped this," I said.

Her eyes went wide. She grabbed the bundle and held it for a moment. "Trash," she said, and then shoved it into the trash bin in the corner. She left and I followed her back to the party.

A few people swatted pearl-colored balloons back and forth with one hand while sipping champagne with the other. Aside from the brief introductions I'd had upon arrival, Cat was the only person at the party I knew. Cat didn't care that I wasn't an industry insider. What she did care about was whether or not I had steady employment, because a fair portion of my disposable income now went back to her store's bottom line. I helped myself to a flute of champagne and weaved through the partygoers looking for her.

I shouldn't have left her alone. In the center of the party by the UP Escalator, Cat stood face to face with her husband, George. A display of gloves, hats, and scarves in bright candy shades provided a nice backdrop. George's lips moved but I was too far away to hear what he said. He looked distraught, earnest. A shock of brown hair had fallen forward on his forehead, making him appear boyish.

In my head, I scripted imaginary dialogue for them. Him apologizing. Her accepting. Him promising to do whatever it would take to get them back on track, her laughing off his fears.

He put his hands on her arms and leaned down and said something to her, and then he stood back up.

And then she grabbed a drink from a passing server and tossed the contents in his face.

3

FRIDAY NIGHT

I held my champagne flute above my head and squeezed through the crowd. By the time I reached Cat, her husband was gone. Party goers had backed up and left a circle of space around her. "Did you see that?" one woman asked. "Hormones," said another, casting a judgmental look at Cat's belly. "I heard she left him for another woman," said a third.

Cat looked stunned. I put my arm around her and led her toward a quiet corner.

"I'm not ready to be a mom. I just threw a drink at the father of my baby! Why did I think I could do this?" Cat said.

"You are going to be a better mom than ninety percent of women who get pregnant. Yes, your life is going to change, but for amazing reasons. You're going to have a baby." I smiled. "That won't change who you are. It's going to magnify who you are."

"You think so?"

"I know so."

Her eyes dropped to my makeshift top and her forehead wrinkled with a frown. "What about you? It would be easier if we did this together. Do you think you'll ever have a baby?"

My nervous system woke up like it had been plugged into an outlet and a cold sweat broke out on the back of my neck. Cat having a baby was one thing. I was pretty sure I knew where I stood on the subject, but the lack of serious relationships had lulled me into a false sense of never having to examine my thoughts too closely.

"Let's get you through your pregnancy before we tackle that issue," I said.

"You're right. You're not even married. Not that you'd have to be..." She looked at me again.

"Let me take care of you while you take care of little Andy or Jenny."

She pulled away. "Isn't that line from *Rosemary's Baby?*"

"We should leave," I said. "Walk with me to the coat check."

Cat turned around and looked at the multitude of faces staring at her. Only a few had the decency to look away. She turned back to me. "I'd rather not. Meet me by the exit?"

"Fine." I went back into the mall and collected our jackets. When I returned, Cat was seated on a low bench with an older man in a tweed suit and a full head of white hair. They appeared to be comfortable with one another. She held a champagne flute, but the beverage was clear. A wedge of lime had settled in the bottom.

"I have the coats," I said, holding them up. "Are you ready to go?"

"Sam, there you are. I want you to meet someone. Jim, this is Samantha Kidd. Sam, this is Jim Insendo. Jim used to own my store," she said.

I shook Jim's hand. "So you're our town sleuth," he said. "I've heard a lot about you. Are you hot on somebody's trail tonight?"

I smiled. "Nope, tonight I'm just a party girl." I looked around the party and spotted the woman from the bathroom standing with George. Maybe there *was* another woman. Things were adding up, but Cat didn't need to know the score. "Come on, we should get you home."

"So soon?"

"I think you should get some rest. It's been a big day."

"Fine," she said. She turned to Jim. "It was nice catching up with you. Call me if you want to get together for coffee. You know the number." She stood up and set her glass on a display of perfumes. Jim smiled, and then stood up and walked to the bar.

"Do you mind if we go to Catnip first? I want to check on the store."

"Fine. I'll meet you there. I need to get something from the bushes outside of the mall."

We both bundled up and left the party. Cat went toward the car and I split off to the right and around the side of the mall in search of my sweater and bra. She passed me as I was pulling dead blades of grass from the knit.

When I reached Catnip, the exterior door was propped open with a rock. I went inside and found Cat straightening a display of colorful cashmere scarves and gloves. "I'm going to get something from my office. I'll only be a minute." She tucked a strand of red hair behind her ear.

"Go do what you have to do. I'm going to the fitting room."

"Don't get distracted. We're only going to be here as long as it takes me to check the safe."

"How long is that?"

"Two minutes."

I could try on at least three outfits in two minutes. I entered the fitting room and stripped down to my fabric tape and panties. Before I had a chance to pull a fringed ivory dress over my head, I heard a crash in the store out front.

4

LATE FRIDAY NIGHT

I peeked out of the dressing room. A figure in baggy black clothes, gloves, and a knit ski mask stood in front of the jewelry case. He held a tire iron in one hand and a handful of thick pearl necklaces in the other. Broken glass was scattered on the floor all around him.

"Hey!" I yelled. I ran out of the fitting room holding the dress in front of me. He took off for the front of the store. Until that moment, I hadn't noticed that the gate wasn't closed.

I ran after him but the lack of support in the ta-ta region slowed me down. Cat stepped out of the shadows and the figure pushed her back. She lost her balance. I changed course and ran to her.

"Are you okay?" I asked. I yanked a blue puffer jacket from a nearby hanger and wadded it up under her back. She put one hand on her tummy. The color had drained from her skin, leaving it a ghostly shade. Her labored breathing came out in bursts like I imagined she'd learned in Lamaze class.

"Did you see what happened?" she asked.

"It was a smash and grab."

"You scared him away. Who knows what he would have done if he didn't see you."

I considered the style in which I'd chased after him: cotton panties and fabric tape. "I don't think he saw me as much of a threat."

A young man in a black uniform ambled up to us. He looked like this job was just his warm up for a night gig as bouncer for the local cover band circuit. His head was clean shaven and shiny—which indicated shaving probably didn't have a lot to do with his choice of hair style. I grabbed another puffer jacket from the fixture and pulled it on over my naked torso.

"Mall's closed, ladies. You need to leave." he said. From our position on the floor, I couldn't tell how tall he was, though his rotund physique made him appear on the short side.

Cat sat up. "This is my store. I'm the owner."

He looked annoyed. "Officer Aguilar. Mall security." He shook Cat's hand and then mine. "I heard a crash. Is everything okay?"

"There was somebody inside her store," I said. "He smashed one of her cases and grabbed her merchandise. He pushed her out of the way when he ran out of the store. That's assault. She's eight months pregnant and could have been hurt. So no, I don't think everything is okay."

That got his attention. He looked back and forth between our faces. "Do you need medical assistance?"

"I'm fine," Cat said. "We were at the party and came here to make sure the store was locked up properly."

"It's after hours. Everybody has to be out by eleven." He looked at Cat. "You know the rules."

"I know," she said.

"The thief was probably already here when we arrived and we just didn't see him," I said. "How would someone get in without you noticing?"

"We try to cover the whole mall, but with that party at the other end, there's a chance someone could have gotten past us. Or maybe they hid in the store after it closed. Were you the one who locked up?"

"No," Cat said. "I didn't even think of what time it was. It's the holidays and since I wasn't the one to lock up, I wanted to check on the store before I went home." Cat sat up and stared at the shattered jewelry case and the broken glass on the carpet. "What do we do now?"

"As long as I'm here we might as well fill out the report." He pulled a radio from his belt and told somebody to override the lights in the rest of the mall. "Show me where this happened."

"I'll go." I stood up and held the puffer jacket closed with my fist. Cat moved from the floor to one of the ottomans that were positioned around the store for customers who needed a rest. Officer Aguilar followed me through the store.

I stuck to the aisles between fixtures. In the darkness, I felt the crunch of broken glass under my feet before I saw it. I grabbed a trash bin from the aisle behind the counter and then stooped down and collected some of the bigger pieces of glass, careful not to cut myself. The lights came on and I blinked a couple of times while my eyes adjusted.

I wished the lights had stayed out.

Because the smash and grab was no longer the issue. Sometime before Cat and I had returned to her store, before I'd ducked into the fitting room for after-hours shopping, before I'd interrupted a robbery in my underwear, Cat's husband the rat had been strangled by a pearl necklace and his body had been left behind the glass case that normally held her jewelry display.

As far as Cat's problems went, this one was on a whole other level.

5

FRIDAY NIGHT: PAST CAT'S BEDTIME

It was a much more official team that worked in Cat's store while we sat, wrapped in blankets, on a nearby ottoman. Emergency technicians had arrived shortly after my call to the police, but there was no urgent pace to their task. George had long since been dead.

By the time the police arrived, I was back in my sweater, camo pants, and proper undergarments. I'd convinced Cat to leave the broken cases as they were.

I knew a few things about crime scene investigation: one, don't touch anything. Fingerprints cast suspicion where I least wanted it. Two, considering my presence at the store, I would be questioned whether I wanted to or not. If lucky, questioning might end up giving me a detail or two. Third, be patient. Eventually, my old pal Detective Loncar would show up. After we caught up on each other's respective lives ("Hi, Detective. Is your wife speaking to you yet?" "Ms. Kidd. Keep out of my investigation."), I'd sit back and watch the routine:

bagging evidence, collecting statements, photographing the surroundings.

It was safe to say we wouldn't be leaving any time soon.

A red-headed young man in a navy blue suit, white shirt, and pink tie approached us. "Which one of you is Catherine Lestes?" He asked

"Me," Cat said.

"I'm Detective Madden. I'd like to ask you a few questions."

"Where's Detective Loncar?" I asked. Madden seemed surprised by my question. "We have a...history," I added.

"Tahiti." He looked at his notebook and then at Cat. "Are you comfortable? Can I get you a cup of water or something before we get started?"

She looked up at him, her eyes wide and red. "Water would be great. Thank you."

"I'll be right back." The detective left us sitting on the ottoman. I was so surprised by his act of generosity that for moment I went blank. And then I remembered it was up to me to coach Cat.

"Listen. He's going to ask you a bunch of questions about tonight. Tell him the truth—"

She interrupted me. "George is gone," she said. "He's really gone. Five hours ago I hated him. I threw a drink in his face. And now he's gone. Forever." Her peaches and cream complexion turned red, and blotchy patches appeared on her throat. She put her hands on her belly and moved them in a circle.

The red-headed detective came back.

"Here he comes. Be cool," I said.

He handed her a small paper cup of water. "Are you okay here on that ottoman? Would you rather move to the sofa? You'll have better back support."

Cat sipped her water. "Thank you. I'm fine here."

I interjected. "Detective, maybe you should talk to me first while Cat calms down."

"Ms. Kidd?" he asked. He looked at his phone. "I'll talk to you in a moment." He was quiet for a few seconds. I imagined him gearing up to go in for the kill now that he'd lulled Cat into a safe space. Instead, he kept his attention on me. "Do you think you could give Ms. Lestes and me a couple of minute alone?"

"I—um—Cat?"

"It's okay, Sam."

"But don't go far. I'd like to talk to you when we're done," Madden added.

"Okay," I said. I stood up and walked away from them, only stopping to turn around and look back twice. Madden sat on the ottoman next to Cat. His head was tipped and if I didn't know any better, I'd say he was laying Good Cop on a little bit thick.

I waited impatiently for my turn to talk to Detective Madden, wandering around the portion of the store that the police had not cordoned off. I bypassed cocktail dresses and headed toward a display of ivory garments. Merchandising an outlet store wasn't as easy as working with new shipments, because the inventory often came in piecemeal. Cat had an exceptional eye for trends, though, and had learned to cherry pick from her inventory to make strong display statements. In front of me, a wall of pale pink slats had been rigged with silver hooks. The dresses varied from ivory to winter white to beige to the palest taupe. Cashmere, wool, tweed, and silk mixed together to create a luxurious display. A neighboring fixture held strands of costume-grade pearls, perfect for achieving the layered look without the investment. An assortment of pearlescent shoes was set up on the corner. I killed time by trying on the shoes. It paid to have sample-sized feet.

"Excuse me, Ms. Kidd?" I turned around. Madden stood in front of me with a clipboard. "Before I get your statement, I want to reassure you that we've been through the store, and there's no longer a threat. Did you sustain any injuries tonight? Would you like to seek medical attention?"

"I'm not the one who got pushed out of the way of a fleeing murderer."

Madden made a note. "Can you tell me what happened here tonight? Just a couple of sentences. In your own words."

"Cat and I came to her store so she could make sure everything was locked up properly. You probably know there've been some smash and grabs in the mall, right?" He nodded once. "We were already here for a party at the end of the mall, so she thought it was best to check before we went home. I was in the fitting room and I heard a crash. When I came out, a person was in front of the jewelry case with a tire iron. When he saw me, he grabbed the jewelry and ran. The mall security officer must have heard the crash, or me yell, or something, because he came in to see what was going on, and that's when we found George's body." I paused. "That was more than a couple of sentences. Sorry."

"That's okay. I want to hear everything you have to say, the whole story. We can take a break if you want." He made a few more notes. "Finding a body is a traumatic situation. Would you like us to call somebody to come pick you up?"

"I'm sorry, do you know who I am?" I asked.

He looked back down at his clipboard. "Ms. Samantha Kidd, right?"

"Right."

"Are you okay?"

"I'm fine. I'll drive Cat—Ms. Lestes—home tonight. You don't have to make special arrangements."

"Would you like some water before you go?"

I felt like I was out to dinner at the Olive Garden, not giving a statement about finding a body. "No, I think I'd really just like to get out of here."

"Fine," he said. "Here's my card. Call me if you think of anything else. Being present at a crime scene is a traumatic situation,"

"You already said that."

"Oh, yes, I did." He looked back down at his clipboard. "Thank you for your statement, Ms. Kidd."

We walked back to where Cat sat in the shoe department. "Ms. Lestes, I'll call you when the forensic team finishes up," Madden said to Cat. "It's going to take us a while to make sure we collect all the evidence. If you think of anything you want to tell me, call me. Here's my card."

Cat took the card and held it in her lap. She looked at the detective. "Thank you," she said. "I'll notify my staff not to come in until I hear from you."

He nodded at her. "Good night, Ms. Lestes, Ms. Kidd."

We walked to the car. Despite the lateness of the hour, Cat called her employees and told them what had happened. It was the worst possible time of the year for a boutique to miss out on business, but the unexpected tragedy had shifted her priorities.

Detective Madden had our names, phone numbers, and statements. There was always the chance that he'd have more questions in a few days, but we'd been forthcoming with our information. The absence of a lecture about not getting involved felt a little strange.

"It's late. Let's get you home and to sleep," I said.

"I can't go to sleep. I have to call my family, and George's family, and then they're going to come visit, and there has to be a memorial, and I don't have groceries, and—"

"Slow down. It's late and you need to go home and try to relax. You can call everybody tomorrow."

Cat put both hands up toward her face and swept her fingers under her eyes to wick away the tears that had pooled there. She tipped her head back and stared at the ceiling, and a fresh wave of tears trickled out of the corners of her eyes and dripped into her hairline by her temples. I felt for her. Here was a woman who appeared in charge of most of the time, and in the past twenty-four hours, life as she knew it had fallen to pieces.

"Sam, can you stay over tonight?" she asked in a small voice.

I thought about every reason I shouldn't: I had no pajamas, toothbrush, or change of clothes for tomorrow. Logan, my trusty feline companion, would be left with dry food and day-old water.

"Of course I can," I said.

I borrowed a pair of PJs and made up the sofa. Cat went to bed. Even though my body was tired, my mind was unsettled. I laid on my side and stared at the mantel above the unlit fireplace. It was filled with framed photos on display, pictures of Cat and George from vacations and cozy nights at home.

There was nothing in George's expression that indicated his unhappiness. Nothing that hinted that this wasn't the life he wanted to lead. His broad smile, body language, and repeated public displays of affection with Cat spoke of the opposite of his actions.

I hated him for tricking her so thoroughly.

Twenty four hours ago, this holiday season had had all the makings of being my best one yet.

Not anymore.

6

SATURDAY, UNGODLY EARLY

I'd like to say that I was the perfect houseguest, waking early and starting breakfast for Cat, but even with the best of intentions, that wasn't the case. Whether or not she was trying to be quiet was a moot point after the shattering of glass woke me from a sound sleep at quarter after five.

"I dropped the coffee pot," she said. The puddles of brown liquid on the floor and the scent of freshly brewed coffee were explanation enough.

"You're not supposed to have caffeine."

"I made it for you."

"Then as a thank you, let me clean it up." She protested but I insisted. "I'll get coffee from the drive through on my way home. It's no big deal."

Cat looked at me for a long moment, and then started to cry. Small sobs at first, which grew into bigger ones. She didn't even bother wiping the tears away this time. Her face turned a shade of red I'd previously only seen in radishes. I scanned the floor for my shoes and pulled them on, and then crossed the floor and hugged her. This time she held on like Molly Brown with a life preserver before climbing aboard Lifeboat No. 6.

We stood like that through the microwave timer and the tea pot whistle. At each domestic sound, I patted Cat on the back and tried to pull away. She gripped me closer.

Seventeen minutes later (microwave clock), she relaxed her arms. I stepped back and appraised her condition. She grabbed a kitchen towel and wiped her face, and then balled up the towel and carried it out of the room leaving dark, coffee-colored footprints in her wake. Good thing she had hardwood floors.

I followed her to the living room and guided her into her favorite chair. "Sit. Relax. I'll take care of the kitchen. You should call your family."

After cleaning the kitchen, resetting the microwave timer, and fixing Cat a mug of green tea, I drove home. I had no problem temporarily moving in with Cat, on one condition. Logan, the most faithful companion a girl could ask for, would move in with me. And assuming I'd woo him with treats, he'd probably agree.

On the drive home, I started a mental list of reasons why George might have been murdered. As morbid as it sounded, it was my way of trying to control an uncontrollable situation. This wasn't the first time I'd found a body. Not even the first time I'd found the body of someone I'd known. But this time, the victim was tied to someone in my life. No matter what the outcome of the ensuing investigation would be, the fact remained that Cat was a widow about to become a single mother.

The first thought to pop into my head was that George had been in the wrong place at the wrong time. But besides that being the answer with the least amount of closure, it also didn't fit. George had gotten into a fight with Cat earlier that night and he'd told her he was leaving her. So what had taken him to her store? Was there more to him leaving her than an untimely mid-life crisis? If it was merchandise he was after, he had access to far more valuable pieces through Kenner & Winn.

Did George have enemies? Or was there a secret that drove him to put distance between himself and Cat in the first place? And the scariest question of all: did his murder have anything to do with Cat, and if so, was she now in danger?

I'd gotten to know Cat over the past two years since first moving to Ribbon. We hadn't been instant friends but a friendship had grown out of our mutual love of clothes. Over that time I became a regular customer of her boutique, and she became an example of what normal people were like. I'd learned early on that her husband's job as a sales rep kept him on the road for about half of the year, which made girl-time the norm.

But for as much time as I'd spent with Cat while George was traveling, I hadn't spent much time with the two of them together and barely knew him at all. The only thing I *did* know was that Cat hadn't taken his last name when they married. It was a decision that had less to do with independence than practicality: George's surname was "Stevens" and Cat preferred not to be confused with the artist formerly known as Cat Stevens.

Traffic around Ribbon had been thinning out gradually as we got closer to Christmas. This morning, the highway was light and I made it home in under the usual twenty minutes. I pulled into my driveway and let myself in.

Logan stood next to his food bowl. He'd tipped the scales at fifteen pounds a few months ago and the vet had put him on a low cal/high fiber diet. When that hadn't worked out,

Logan and I reached an agreement. He could have the kind of cat food he wanted, but only a half portion. In a show of solidarity I did my best to do the same, but between you and me, eating half a pizza isn't all that different from eating the whole thing.

I scooped half a can of high protein fish parts into Logan's bowl and called my best friend Eddie at Tradava, the local department store and our joint employer. Eddie was a surfer-dude type who maintained a go-with-the-flow vibe on most occasions. He was as at home on a skateboard as he was in his VW Bug, but I'd never seen him as stressed out as he'd been during the holidays. For the past month, his vocabulary had more expletives than *Scarface*.

According to the clock, he'd be somewhere between his second and third cups of coffee. "I shouldn't even take your call," he said in place of hello. "Vacation the week before Christmas while I'm stuck here round the clock. Last night a tree fell over and pinned Santa. Destroyed three of the elves. I had to replace them with garden gnomes. If the store manager sees that, I'm done."

"Good morning to you too," I said. "Have you heard from Cat?"

"No. Why? She didn't go into labor early, did she?"

"Her situation is a little more dire than premature labor. Her husband was murdered last night."

"I have seven minutes. Talk fast."

I told Eddie everything I knew. "He left her yesterday. Like—left her, left her. Said he couldn't do the whole start-a-family thing, that he wasn't ready. She was freaking out, smashing plates, full on Connie Corleone from *The Godfather*. We crashed his party at the mall and they fought, but then later when we went to her store he was there. Dead. Behind a jewelry case with a strand of pearls from her inventory tied around his throat."

"I think I missed something. He had a party last night but was dead in her store? How'd he get from the party to her store?"

"You told me to talk fast so I edited."

"So you don't know how long he was gone? Or when he left? Or how he got there?"

"We don't know anything except the fact that he was in her store, strangled with a strand of pearls."

"Whoa. What did Detective Loncar say?"

"Apparently he's on vacation. It was weird. The detective we spoke with was named Madden. He acted like everything was routine."

"You found the body and called 911?"

"Yes."

"Sounds routine to me."

"It's not like I expected a gold star but a little positive reinforcement wouldn't hurt."

"Dude."

"Okay, fine. I feel like Loncar and I have an agreement."

"You do. You agree to stay out of his investigations and he doesn't arrest you for obstruction of justice."

"That was last year. I think we had a breakthrough around my birthday."

We were silent for a moment. "I don't envy her," Eddie said. "The holidays are rough for any retailer. Even in quote-unquote normal cities the crime rate rises. At least once a year there's a shooter dressed in a Santa costume on the news. People are shopping under pressure, employees are burned out, and stores are fighting for every sale we can get. It's not pretty."

It had started as a subtle shift, one that some stores never saw coming. Buyers, like I'd been when I worked in New York, had been the ones to determine what a store would carry. In a way, we were style curators, editing a designer's collection down from a sea of samples into a cohesive assortment that we felt our customers would want. But designers soon learned that if they embraced the internet, they could offer their entire collection to the world and let customers—*not* store buyers—make the decisions of what would be produced. Ready-to-wear, a market that could shift quickly, found it more profitable to go direct to consumer and cut out the retailers. The accessories market had it harder because of materials and factory production schedules.

The changing face of retail meant good things for customers but not so stable for stores. In the simplest terms of supply and demand, the scales had been tipped in the wrong direction. Profit, the money between what a store charged for an item minus the various costs of doing business, had been whittled down to pennies. The easiest way to make a profit was to lower the cost of an item.

Ribbon, Pennsylvania was the first city to have outlet malls. But the one where Cat worked, the Designer Outlet Mall, had been different. It wasn't the kind that had been around since the fifties, offering girdles and surplus glassware and dungarees. It was the kind that promoted in-season trends and designer merchandise with the understanding that you'd pay less than if you shopped at a store like Tradava.

But places like Tradava weren't exactly pulling in hordes of customers anymore. A tough economy had caused most customers to tighten their belts—or stop buying belts to begin with. Subsequently, the retail stores slashed prices, and the outlet malls were no longer unique. Finding a way to gain a portion of a customer's wallet had gotten tougher than ever. It was part of my new challenge in the advertising department. How to promote the same trends that everybody else promoted while creating customer loyalty? Difficult, but not impossible.

"Do you think the murder is connected to the outlets?" Eddie asked.

"It's hard not to see the connection. Eddie, I'm worried. Cat's pregnant and hormonal and her business is at risk and now this. Logan and I are staying with her for a few days. I don't think she should be alone right now."

7

SATURDAY MORNING

I dressed in a cream cable knit turtleneck sweater, cream corduroy trousers with pale pink suede knee patches, and pink lizard boots. I blow-dried my hair into a soft bob and filled an empty suitcase with enough clothes to get me into the new year. The doorbell rang as I was sitting on top of the suitcase to get it to zip. I ran downstairs and answered the door. A man in a FedEx uniform stood on my porch.

"Samantha Kidd?"

"That's me."

"Sign here." He shoved a black device at me and I signed the screen with a thin black plastic wand. The signature wasn't anywhere close to my own. He took the equipment and handed me a box. "Have a nice day." He turned and left.

I stared at the package. It was from the Apple store. I held it up to my head. It wasn't ticking. (It's good to be cautious.) Logan rubbed his back against my ivory pant legs, leaving a transfer of black fur on my shins. He looked up at me and meowed.

"We'll leave in a second." I pushed the door shut behind me and tore open the box.

Whatever I expected, a new iPhone wasn't it. I powered it on. There was one message from the only number programmed in: The Charming and Handsome Nick Taylor.

I bit back a smile. I wasn't a hundred percent on board with the Amanda Ries Roommate situation, but Nick got points for making me laugh. I cued up the message.

"Hey, Kidd, It's Nick." There was a slight pause. "Call me when you get a chance, okay? I don't like how things ended last night."

I pressed redial. One ring, two rings, three rings, four rings...

It was a little after seven. Six hour time difference meant it was a little after one in Italy. The phone rang. And rang. And rang. As I was about to hang up, he answered.

"Nick? It's Samantha. I was hoping to catch you alone." I paused, cringing at the words spilling out of my mouth. "Not that I think you're not alone. Or are. I mean, there are a lot of Italians in Italy, so you're probably not alone."

"Kidd, slow down."

"Okay." I took a deep breath. "Hi."

"Hi. You got the phone."

"I got the phone."

"Before I left you mentioned something about wanting to upgrade. Consider it an early Christmas present. Your personal private, direct line to me. Whenever you want to talk. No matter what's going on, if you call, I'll answer."

"Don't answer if you're in the bathroom." He laughed. I turned and walked toward the sofa. "'The Charming and Handsome Nick Taylor?'"

"I may have been overselling."

40

"No, I think it fits." I sat down. "How'd you program me?"

"If only I could program you."

"You know what I mean. Is my number in your phone?"

"Yes. 'That Crazy Broad.'"

"You did not."

"You'll just have to wait until we're in the same city to find out, won't you?" He was quiet for a second. "Kidd, I'm sorry about last night. Are you okay with this?" he asked. "With Amanda staying here?"

Last night. Thirteen hours ago I'd put Nick in the same category as Cat's husband: men are rats. I thought about last night, about finding George's dead body at her store. Hours before he'd been found dead they'd fought, first at home and then at the party. Their differences had been over something far greater than letting a friend crash on his sofa. In terms of things to be angry about, this one was pretty small.

"I kind of have to be, don't I?"

"It would make things a lot easier if you were."

"Okay," I said with more conviction than I felt. "What about your dad? Do you need me to check in on him?"

"If you saw how he keeps the place when I'm not there, you might be scared away for good. Between you and me, he might have met a lady friend at the grocery store. Better give them their space."

"If that's the case, then we'll have a whole new set of problems when you get back."

"We'll figure it out. I know we both thought I'd be home by now. I really am sorry about the timing."

"It's okay, I understand. You're lucky the factories weren't closed."

"I had to call in a couple of favors. If I don't meet with them now, I'll lose a month of production." He paused. "So, we're good?"

"We are, but there's somebody who isn't." I chewed my lower lip for a second. Telling Nick about things of this nature hadn't been easy in the past, but I knew that not telling Nick would be worse. "You remember Cat Lestes, right? Her husband, George, died last night."

"Isn't she about to have a baby? That's beyond tragic. Was it stress? Heart attack?"

"No, Nick, it was murder." I left out the details about their fight and George telling Cat he was leaving her. "We found his body in her store."

Nick was silent. There was an ocean between us, but that didn't matter. I half expected a lecture and half expected him to hang up.

"Be careful, Kidd. I mean that. I know Cat's your friend and I know your friends are like your family. And I know you're going to be there to help her through this. Just be careful, okay? Promise me that?"

"I'll be careful. I promise."

After our call, I packed Logan up in the car and returned to Cat's house. A short woman in a black wool coat and red scarf with snowflakes printed on it was leaving as I arrived. Cat was inside on the sofa, wrapped in a pink fleece blanket. Logan crawled out of his carrier, jumped up next to her, and curled up in the blanket folds.

"Who was that woman?" I asked.

"One of my neighbors. She saw the news and came by to drop off some food."

A shiny white plate filled with square cut brownies sat on the glass coffee table in front of her. Small ceramic dessert plates sat next to the tray. "She brought you brownies?"

"She brought me a casserole. The fourth one today."

"You've had four visitors already? It's eight o'clock in the morning."

"I've been up since five. I needed junk food so I made brownies after you left. Help yourself." I reached for a dessert plate and stacked two brownies on it. "The doctor wants me to eat more vegetables, so there's spinach and cooked carrots in them."

I put one of the brownies back. "How are you feeling?" I asked. "Any better? Any differently?"

"Better, maybe. I don't think I can cry anymore. Differently, I don't know. My parents are on their way from Florida, and George's family called this morning to find out when the memorial service will be. The phones won't stop ringing so I turned them off. I've already gotten five emails from Fidelity about what to do with George's 401K. It's like an automated machine. 'loved one dies—initiate sequence five.'" She wrapped the blanket around her a little tighter and Logan meowed. "I feel like a fraud. He left me, Sam. He walked away from me and our marriage. Yesterday I hated him for what he did, and today everybody's suffocating me with what a great guy he was and how sorry they are that I lost the love of my life. I feel like I'm lying to everybody by not telling them that our marriage was over."

"Cat, I need to ask you something." She looked up at me. "What did George say to you at the party that made you throw your drink at him?"

"He told me to go home. He said considering the circumstances, I was making a fool of myself. And then he threatened me. He said if I expected anything from him in the future, I needed to stay out of his business. I know throwing the drink was childish. I didn't even think about it. I was so angry with him I wanted to spit in his face!" Her eyes grew wide and she clamped her hand over her mouth. Logan let out a long, low growl, as if he didn't like the direction the conversation had taken.

I picked Logan up and cradled him against my arm. I stroked the fur on his belly, which was still rather large thanks to the overeating situation. He closed his eyes halfway and purred.

"You had every right to be mad at him, and throwing a drink was a lot nicer than spitting in his face." Logan opened his eyes and meowed again. "I know what happened. You know what happened. But the rest of the world doesn't have to know. People want to support you right now so let them. You need to let me help you. Except for some last minute Christmas shopping, my schedule is clear."

Unlike Eddie, who'd been fighting a losing battle of merchandising standards vs. customer shopping destruction, *Retrofit for Tradava* had put the spring/summer issue to bed two weeks ago and my last minute request for time off the week prior to Christmas had been approved by the director of marketing.

Merry Christmas to me.

"I can't expect you to spend your first real vacation helping me at my store. Not the week before Christmas." She ran her hand over Logan's head. "Besides, I already made arrangements for help."

"You hired someone to help with the funeral planning?"

"No. I called my brother."

8

SATURDAY MORNING

Cat's brother Dante had made more of an impact on me than I would have expected. Between the two of us, Cat was the normal one. My friendship with her had grown from when we'd first met during a design competition, to our joint participation in a local publicity stunt, to my becoming a regular customer at her designer boutique. I'd had a brief flirtation with Dante during my breakup with Nick, though Cat had appeared not to care either way that the flirtation had been short-lived.

It didn't seem appropriate to ask the questions that sprung to mind: when is he coming? Where is he staying? Does my hair look okay? Especially since I was in a relationship with The Charming and Handsome Nick Taylor and had only recently shown great maturity and acceptance about the fact that he was sharing his apartment with Amanda.

I temporarily forgot about the vegetables in the brownie and ate it. It was surprisingly good. I reached for the plate and picked up another. There was a shave-and-a-haircut rap on the door. A couple of seconds later, a familiar voice spoke. "C'mon, Sis, I don't have all day."

Cat left the blanket on the sofa and answered the door. "It's about time you got here," she said.

Dante entered. He wore his trademark black leather motorcycle jacket over a faded zip front hoodie and T-shirt. His black hair was pushed away from his face, and his normally long sideburns had recently been trimmed. He carried a casserole dish covered in clear plastic wrap in one hand and a large black canvas bag slung over the other shoulder. Cat shut the door behind him. He dropped the bag on the floor.

Dante was a freelance photographer who occasionally picked up hours working for a private investigator. His background was slightly blurry: never been married, worked odd jobs, lived in Philadelphia. He was a flirt, a willing participant in my sometimes ill-conceived investigations, and a really good kisser. When Nick and I talked about Dante, it was mostly about the private investigator stuff. Otherwise we veered into the same territory as when we talked about Amanda.

Dante showed no surprise at seeing me. "Hold this." He shoved the casserole at me. When I took it, he turned to Cat and wrapped her in a giant, brotherly hug. "You okay?" He asked. Her head nodded against his shoulder.

When their hug ended, Cat took the casserole from me and went to the kitchen.

"So, Sammy the Kidd. How's your boyfriend?"

"He's good. We're good. Everything's good."

"Good."

46

"What about you? Everything good?" I asked. My vocabulary was going to require a good-ectomy if this kept up.

"Truth? I've been a little lonely."

"Somehow I doubt that."

He shrugged. "Believe what you want."

Dante was baiting me. He'd crashed my life about two years ago and had been in and out ever since. I'm not going to lie. There was some serious chemistry.

But.

Yes, I was attracted to Dante. He was equal parts Marlon Brando and Adrian Zmed. (Don't even pretend you haven't seen *Grease 2*. You know what I'm talking about.) He was the stereotypical bad boy dressed in a black leather motorcycle jacket and tattoos. Except as I got to know him, I realized he was anything but stereotypical.

Dante kept me on my toes during the time we were together, but showed me that we could connect on a deeper level too. We shared a bed but didn't sleep together. He told me about his son. I told him about my fears. It was an exciting week that opened up my world a little more than when life was about my career as a former shoe buyer and my ongoing flirtation with Nick. It gave me a taste of what life with Dante would be like.

Maybe that's why I ended things. I wasn't a hundred percent confident that anybody could have a life with Dante. He was a loner.

Dante could throw his belongings into a backpack and ride his motorcycle into the sunset. That wasn't the life for me, but the short time I'd spent close to his flame had made me view my own life differently. I'd confronted the issues that had kept me from finding steady employment. I took the rose-colored glasses off and examined my life and saw what it was that I wanted.

Logan walked the length of the sofa and then jumped onto the floor and sniffed the bag that Dante had dropped. Dante scooped Logan up and scratched his ears. Within seconds, Logan purred like a lawnmower engine.

"I missed your cat," Dante said.

"Sounds like he missed you too."

He carried Logan to a large club chair and sat down. "Okay, sis, what's the plan?" he called out.

Cat came back from the kitchen and sat down. "I don't have a plan. My whole life is falling apart and I'm trying to hold it together."

Dante looked at me. "I almost hate to ask this question, but do you have a plan?"

"I'm more of a first-things-first strategist."

"Okay, so what's the first thing we need to tackle?"

Cat replied. "Your priority is the store. Detective Madden called and said they released the crime scene." Cat's complexion turned a shade of green. "I'll be right back." She jumped up from the sofa and ran down the hall to the bathroom. Even though she slammed the door, it wasn't hard to guess what she was doing. (I only hoped it had to do with the pregnancy or the thought of her store as crime scene and not the vegetable-laced brownies.)

I looked at Dante. "How much do you know?" I asked him.

"Not much. Talk fast."

"George told her he was leaving her yesterday morning. She didn't take it well. We went to his company holiday party last night. They got into a fight in front of a lot of people and then we left."

"And his body was found in her store later that night."

"Yes. When we got there, we thought we were alone, but we weren't. Somebody dressed in all black was there to rob the store."

"Burgle."

"What?"

"Robbers rob people. Burglars rob stores. The store was closed, so it was a burglar, not a robber."

"Whatever. I don't know if it was a man or a woman but I keep thinking it was a man. He smashed the jewelry case with a tire iron."

"Did he see you?"

I nodded. "I heard the crash and saw him. I yelled and he took off. He shoved Cat out of the way and ran out the front gate."

Dante set Logan down and balled up his fist, and then slammed it into the back of Cat's brown leather club chair. Logan jumped down from the sofa and ran under the couch. I knew Dante was angry. I also knew he usually bottled stuff like that up and that the reaction I'd just seen would be his only one. Frankly, I was a little surprised he'd reacted that much.

"I keep replaying things in my mind but the only thing I remember clearly is that the thief was just standing there staring at the jewelry case. When I yelled, he grabbed the jewelry and took off."

"Why don't you know if it was a man or a woman?"

"He—or she—was wearing baggy black clothes, a ski mask, and gloves."

"Could have been a burglary gone wrong. Could be the burglar snapped and killed George in some kind of trance. Your yell snapped him out of it."

I shook my head. "I could see that if it was a gunshot or a head wound but it takes a lot of effort to strangle somebody with a necklace and then drag their body behind a jewelry case. And the necklaces would only be strong enough if they were doubled over, so that requires a little more effort. This feels more deliberate."

"That does sound deliberate."

The door in the hall opened and Cat came out. Her lipstick was faded to a ring of faint burgundy around the outside of her mouth. Her red hair was pulled back into a high ponytail that had already come loose and was tipped slightly to the side.

"Sam, can you pack up the brownies? I don't really want to deal with them after," she pointed behind her "that."

"Sure." I carried the tray of brownies into the kitchen and found a plastic food container and a corresponding lid. I packed all but two away and opened the fridge. The shelves were overflowing with glass dishes filled with casseroles. I did a little rearranging and then tucked the vegetable brownies in the lunch meat drawer. The way things were going, I had a chance of hitting the recommended vegetable intake for one day and I wasn't going to blow it.

I rejoined Cat and Dante in the living room. He'd moved to the sofa next to her and had his hand on her back. "Are you sure?" she asked.

"You need to take care of yourself," he said. "We'll take care of the store."

"We?" I asked.

Dante looked at me. "Yes, we." He stood up. "Cat's going to the doctor and we're going to the outlet to clean up the crime scene."

We took separate cars. Dante drove a black SUV filled with vacuum cleaners and miscellaneous boxes of rags and jugs of chemicals. I took my late Nineties black Honda del Sol, a hard-top convertible with ridiculously low mileage thanks to the fact that for the majority of the nine years I worked in New York, it sat in a parking garage. My car was considerably zippier than Dante's SUV and I left him in my dust.

The mall was hopping with holiday shoppers. I found a space at the perimeter of the lot and approached the building. Cat had given me the keys to Catnip, but I hadn't forgotten that on two separate occasions criminals had gotten inside when the store was locked. I was curious about the condition the police had left the place, but not so foolish that I charged inside without Dante. I waited on the sidewalk for a couple of minutes until his black SUV pulled up to the curb.

"Help me unload then I'll park and we can go inside." He climbed out and met me around the back.

"What'd you do—rob a sanitation service?" I asked.

"The PI I sometimes work for had me do crime scene cleanup," he said. "Good way to get first access to a crime scene. Cops do their thing, but you never know what else you can find. Sometimes you can tell where the cops focused their attention. Wait too long and you learn nothing."

"There are people who make their living doing this."

"And they're good. Too good when you're looking for evidence or clues. That's why it's best to do it yourself." He pulled two shiny vacuum cleaners out of the truck. One of them still had a tag on it.

"These look brand new," I said.

"They are. Crime scenes can be messy. Depending on what's at the scene, you won't want to waste time trying to clean up a vacuum. Easier to toss them when you're done."

I paused with one hand on the handle of the vacuum and a box of heavy black garbage bags under my arm. "How messy?"

"You said George was strangled, right? So we're lucky. It's a black bag job. No hazardous waste." He looked down at my feet. "You're wearing pink lizard boots."

"Do you like them?"

"They're not practical."

"I didn't know I was going to be cleaning a crime scene."

He pulled out his wallet and handed me a twenty. "Go to the camping store next door and buy a pair of sneakers."

"I can afford a new pair of sneakers," I said (proudly). "Besides, I don't think twenty dollars would cover it."

"Don't get caught up in what they look like. Go cheap."

"I don't wear cheap shoes."

"You're going to throw them out too."

"That's not how people are supposed to approach the purchase of new shoes."

Dante rolled his eyes. "I'll unload into the store. Meet me back here."

I walked to the mall entrance and then continued on to the camping store. An announcement came over the loudspeaker reminding customers of the gift wrap stations throughout the mall. I asked a guy who looked like he'd been camping in the mountains for weeks before starting his shift for the location of the sneakers and was sent to the back corner. I found the clearance aisle facing the back wall and snatched a pair of marked down rubber rain boots.

Twenty dollars. Sold.

I carried them to the checkout station. The mountain man waved me to his register. Up close, his look was more Hipster Hunter than authentic. A buffalo plaid shirt was buttoned up to his chin and half tucked in. The fray on his jeans appeared carefully placed, not achieved through wear and tear. Elmer Fudd couture, I thought.

I looked around the store. "Have you seen any mall security officers? I need to talk to them." I asked.

Hipster Hunter scanned my items. "Why? Don't tell me you forgot where you parked your car. How do people forget where they parked their cars?"

"No, it's about what happened at the mall last night. Were you working? Did you see or hear anything?"

Hipster stopped scanning barcodes and studied me. He shook his head. "My night off. I heard about it this morning. Wild."

I yessed and no'd my way through the transaction, turning down add-on items in order to get out of there faster. I knew the task ahead of Dante and me would be both time consuming and unpleasant, but I couldn't help wonder if we'd find something amongst the cleared crime scene that would help us shed light on who had murdered George.

9

SATURDAY MID-MORNING

After I paid, I changed from my pink lizard boots into the rain boots. I walked back to Catnip through the warmth of the interior. The gate was down, making the store appear out of business at a time when the rest of the mall was thriving. An empty glass and chrome fixture sat outside the gate. It was a display case just like the one that had been smashed last night: rectangular with glass on the top, front, and sides. Chrome trim. Blond wood trim around the base and on the lockable drawers on the back. The drawers were unlocked and a set of keys were inside in a clear plastic bag, taped to the base with masking tape. More masking tape was wound around the outside of the case several times, and CATNIP had been written on the tape in sloppy handwriting. I left the mall and doubled back to the outside entrance and knocked. Dante opened the door.

"All set?" Dante asked.

"I guess. The new jewelry fixture is on the other side of the gate."

"First we clean. Take this," he said. He rolled a large Hepa-Vac toward me. "Concentrate on getting up what's left of the broken glass. The police got most of it but the jewelry counter is right across the aisle from her shoe department. Cat won't want to take any chances on somebody accidentally stepping on glass with a bare foot."

"The police vacuumed? That was considerate."

"Trace evidence. That's the easiest way to make sure they don't leave a clue behind."

My heart sank. "We're not going to find anything that they didn't, are we?"

"Is that why you're here? You thought you were going to find something they missed?"

"I'm here for Cat."

"But if you happened to pick up a clue that the police left behind, you'd be okay with that."

"Well, duh."

"Forget that. Police are only that dumb on TV. Our job is to get the store looking like Cat wants the store to look. So first, we go over everything again to make sure it's clean and safe. Then I'll replace the broken fixture so you can merchandise it. What the police did do was leave behind coffee cups. Throw them out. Pretend this is your store and you have to get it ready for business."

"Got it." I dragged the Hepa-VAC with me to the area where the case had been smashed, stashed my boots next to the shopping bags, and got started.

I needn't have worried about time spent with Dante. He went one direction and I went the other. As suspected, the store was littered with used white disposable cups. I found an empty roll of trash bags in a drawer behind the register and searched the store for cups like I was a kid at an Easter Egg Hunt. Once I was sure I'd disposed of them all, I knotted the bag and set it by the front gate next to the rest of the store trash.

After coffee cup duty I moved on to vacuuming. I worked by the store entrance. The gate between the entrance and the mall was in place, keeping our activities out of view from customers. I could hear the sounds of holiday shopping through the gate: snippets of conversation, the rhythm of footsteps passing by, and the occasional melody from the soundtrack that had been playing since the week before Thanksgiving. The news about George had been released and I was glad we were behind the metal gate. Knowing how people rubbernecked at accidents along the side of the road, I could only imagine what they were whispering about the murder that had taken place inside of Catnip.

A couple of hours in, I took a break in the stockroom and brewed a pot of coffee. Clean plates for employee use had been stacked on a shelf next to the cups. I moved them to a more secure area, poured two mugs of coffee, and went back to the store. Dante rested against the wrap stand inside the jewelry cases. I handed him a mug.

"How's it going?" I asked.

"Police left the store better than I expected. We're lucky the gate keeps us hidden from the rest of the mall. This would take twice as long if we had spectators." He took a pull on his coffee. "What are your theories?"

"About what?"

"About what happened here."

"What makes you think I have theories?"

"You always have theories."

"Okay fine, I have theories. Do you want to take five and bounce them around?"

Dante raised his eyebrow slightly but didn't answer. I took it as a yes.

"Cat doesn't usually carry expensive jewelry. The merchandise that was stolen, that was an experiment. And not just any experiment. The merchandise came from George's company, Kenner & Winn. In the ten years that Cat and George were together, it was the first time she placed an order with him from any of the vendors he represented. She said he told her another account canceled the order, so he could sell it to her cheap—he actually convinced her to take the merchandise."

"So there's a connection to his employer and to another retail account."

"Yes. His employers would have known the merchandise was in Cat's store, at least, I assume there'd be a paper trail through invoices. Maybe the other retail account, too. It helps explain the theft, but not the murder."

"Who do you suspect for the murder?"

"You know how I am. I suspect everybody."

He smiled. "What else?"

"Someone on her staff could have been involved. It would be easy enough for one of them to make a copy of the key to get in after hours. And George—I can't help wondering about the timing of their fight. I agree with Cat—he was a rat for leaving her while she's eight months pregnant with his baby—but it had to take courage for him to speak up at all. He does what might have been the hardest thing of his life and then gets killed hours later. The timing seems suspicious. Did you know him? I mean, he was married to your sister. Did you see any of this coming?"

"I knew him, but not well. Holidays, mostly, and there was drinking involved. Seemed nice enough and got along with the family. He made my sister happy, but I know she wished he was around more. What about you?"

"I never knew George because he was always traveling. Cat said he'd only been with the jewelry company for a couple of months. I thought maybe he changed companies so he wouldn't have to travel as much."

"You said George was at the party. Notice anything strange?" He leaned forward on the jewelry case. I stood opposite him on the outside. If the store had been open, it would look like he was trying to sell me something.

"At one point Cat and George spoke. It looked like things were going to be civil, but then Cat grabbed a drink and tossed it in his face." I closed my eyes for a moment to recall the scene. "Later, before we left, I saw him talking to a woman in a yellow strapless dress with red accessories." I opened my eyes. "I notice stuff like that."

"What does it mean to you?"

"I don't know."

"Yes, you do. You noticed her for a reason and I'm guessing it's not because you're a fan of the ketchup and mustard color palette."

I thought back to the first time I'd seen her. "She and I were in the bathroom at the same time. She dropped something. I picked it up and handed it to her and she threw it into the trash. Later, George was off to the side talking to her. My first thought was that the real reason George left Cat was that he was having an affair with her, but their body language didn't fit."

"Why did you two come here after the party?"

"One of Cat's employees quit after her shift was over and Cat was afraid she didn't lock up properly. I wanted to get her out of the party without seeing George talking to the woman in yellow. We came here and interrupted the theft in progress. Right after the crash I yelled and scared the robber-burglar-person. He practically knocked Cat over when he ran out of the store."

He stood up straight and balled his fists. "She could have been hurt."

"I know. What I don't know is if the burglar knew she was pregnant. The lights were out and she had her coat on. If it was somebody who knew her, then they would have known she was. If it was random or someone hired to do it, they would have only thought that she was in the way of their exit."

"Either way it's assault."

We were interrupted by the sound of someone rapping on the outside of the metal gate by the mall entrance. I followed Dante to the front of the store. Pieces of mail had been pushed under the gate and spread out in a display of light blue, pink, and white envelopes. The rapping started again, followed by a voice.

"Mall security. Anybody in there? You gotta get this case out of the way."

Dante stepped over the envelopes on the floor. "Hold on. I'll open the gate."

I handed him the keys. He tried a few until one fit into the box. He flipped the handle to the left and the gate chugged and retracted. When it was halfway up, he turned the handle to the right. The gate stopped.

The mall was filled with customers. A few stopped what they were doing to watch us. Two women in matching pink knit hats with pompoms on top stood by a sign that advertised free gift wrap with purchases over a hundred dollars. One of them said, "Is that the store?" The other said yes. Dante'd been right. If we'd had spectators while we were putting the store back together, it would have taken a lot longer.

Fortunately for us, the fixture was on castors. Dante ducked under the gate and pushed it into the store. The weight of the fixture caused it to sway to the left. I stood backward on the opposite side and guided it so it stayed on the marble path. Once we were inside, Dante grabbed the bottom of the metal gate and pulled down. It didn't budge.

"You two get that fixture in place. I'll watch the entrance," the security officer said.

"Let's go." We maneuvered the fixture down the aisle and past a table loaded with cashmere sweaters. It took a little effort to move it once it was on the carpet, but with one of us at either end, we were able to slowly nudge it into place. Dante left me to merchandise. About half a minute later, I heard the gate chug back into place.

For the rest of the afternoon, I worked on a new display in the jewelry department. Like most retailers, Cat kept her back stock locked in drawers behind the fixtures. What people often didn't realize was that vendors shipped merchandise in unglamorous plastic bags and sent velvet boxes and cleaning cloths separately. I unlocked and relocked four different drawers before I found the bags of pearl jewelry. The items were sorted by color in large freezer bags, and individual pieces were in smaller bags within.

I unpacked several thirty-six inch strands of dull black pearls, and then matching bracelets, earrings, and rings. Another drawer search netted me display props: a mauve flocked velvet neck stand to show off a three-strand Jackie Kennedy-styled necklace, a slightly inclined rectangular platform on which to arrange the long strand of pearls, and a couple of matching four inch square pillows that I hooked the bracelets around. Earrings went on earring stands and rings on ring holders. When I finished fitting everything into the display, I moved to the front to see if my angles were all straight. That was the first of seven attempts before I felt I'd achieved ninety-degree perfection.

Occasionally the scents of chocolate and cinnamon floated past me. Even though Cat's gate was in place, it was hard to get away from the ambiance.

By the time I finished, the cases were full with a meticulously placed assortment of pearl necklaces, bracelets, and earrings. It wasn't the valuable merchandise that Cat had planned to display, but a part of me wanted to see if a smash and grab happened again tonight—*after* the murder—and if the thieves really knew the value of what they were stealing. All pearls look lustrous by night, even the knock-offs.

I locked what was left of the back stock in a drawer behind the counter and went looking for Dante. I found him outside Cat's office. "Are you ready to leave?"

"One last thing to do. Install a camera."

"The mall has cameras."

"Outside, and we won't be able to see what they see. This way, we'll have our own surveillance." He went inside the office and I followed.

Retail store space, when empty, was basically a giant box. Profitability was estimated by the square foot, and after taking out stockroom and fitting room space, there was little left for Cat. Her office was about eight feet square, with a tall filing cabinet set up along the wall she shared with the camping store next door. Bookcases filled with catalogs and binders of sales figures lined the back wall. Two chairs rounded out the furniture assortment: one behind and one in front of the wooden desk. Add in Dante and me, and the quarters were very, very close.

Dante dropped a duffle bag onto the chair in front of the desk. After unzipping it, he pulled out a couple of computer tablets.

"What are you going to do with those?" I asked.

"Program them to take pictures every five minutes. We'll see if there's anything suspicious going on around here."

"But you won't know if anything happens until you take them down and look at the pictures. By then the damage will be done."

He propped himself up against the desk. "If we want to find out who's doing something they shouldn't be doing, this is the best way to do it. We're not in this to strike back. If security was doing their job, this never would have happened." He tapped the screen a couple of times. "For all we know, they might be in on it."

"Okay, so what do we do with it?"

He finished tapping and handed me the tablet. "Put this on the second shelf so it's aimed at the door."

I held out my hand, and he set the tablet in my palm. When his fingers brushed mine a shock passed between us. We both pulled away and the tablet fell to the carpet.

It landed right next to my rubber rain boot. He stooped to pick it up. I couldn't help but notice how close he was to my legs. When he stood back up he glanced down to my pink suede knee patches on my pants, then up to my face.

He handed the tablet to me again. I went behind Cat's desk and climbed on top of it, and then positioned the tablet on top of the filing cabinet. I arranged a plastic plant on one side and a short stack of catalogs on the other, hoping to conceal everything but the lens. I probably fiddled with it longer than necessary because I was going to have to ask Dante's help to get down and wanted to postpone that moment as long as possible.

"I think it's in place." I turned to face him, but was still standing on the chair. "Can you help me?"

"Sure."

I expected him to hold out a hand and guide me to the floor. I didn't expect him to wrap an arm around my knees and throw me over his shoulder.

He carried me out of Cat's office and then bent down and lowered me onto a large tufted ottoman. I pulled my sweater down and smoothed the creases out of my corduroys. Dante seemed to enjoy my embarrassment a little too much.

"The tablet will take a picture every five minutes for twenty four hours."

Without stopping to do the math I exclaimed, "That's like a thousand pictures!"

"Two hundred eighty-eight per tablet."

He went into the office and returned with an empty duffel bag. We moved the cleaning equipment to the exit. Dante pulled the SUV the curb and we packed everything in the back.

"My car's in the back row," I said.

"Climb in. I'll give you a ride."

He drove to my small convertible, sandwiched between two minivans. They hadn't left much space for me to get in or out, but that wasn't my primary concern.

No, I was more concerned with the knife protruding from the now completely flat back tire. Suddenly Cat's troubles didn't seem so unique.

10

SATURDAY EVE

The two of us stared at my tire. I didn't know what Dante was thinking, but the thoughts running through my head were built of a string of profanities that would have made Eddie proud.

"Call the police," Dante said.

"The police? They're not going to change my tire."

"I'll change your tire."

"I can change my own tire."

"I'm sure you can. And I'm almost willing to say yes and let you freeze your butt off because it's sometimes fun to watch you think you can do everything yourself, but it's late, this is vandalism, and we need to get back to check on my sister. So you call the police and I'll get started on the tire."

"You wouldn't believe how polite the cops were the night we found George. Watch this. I bet they offer to come out and give me a ride home." I pulled the Nick Phone out of my handbag and called the police. "I'd like to report an act of vandalism."

"In progress?"

"No, in my tire. Somebody stuck a knife in my tire."

"Is the perpetrator still there?"

"No. I came out to my car and there was a knife in the tire."

"At your residence?"

"No, at the Ribbon Designer Outlets."

"You can fill out a police report online. Do you have a pen?"

"A pen? For what?"

"I'll give you the website address."

"I'll find it on my own." I hung up. "Something's up with the police department," I said to Dante.

"Why? Are they treating you like a law-abiding citizen?"

"I am a law-abiding citizen." I shoved the phone into my pocket. "Why don't you just drop me off at Cat's? I'll deal with the car tomorrow."

He stood up and studied me. "How come you're not spending the night with your boyfriend? Trouble in paradise?"

"Paradise is great. Nick's in Italy. I told Cat I'd stay with her for a couple of days."

"Sounds like we'll be getting cozy."

"'We'? I thought you kept an apartment in Ribbon."

"I sublet it to a couple visiting from France." A flicker of a smile twitched at his lips. "Sounds like the makings of a slumber party."

"Change of plans." I held out my keys. "You can change the tire and then go stay at my house."

"It makes a lot more sense for you to go home and for me to stay with my sister."

"My cat is at her house. Home is where your cat is."

We exchanged keys. "You don't trust yourself around me," he said.

"You tell yourself whatever you have to so you can get through the night."

I didn't wait around to "help" him. I started the engine and pulled out of the space. As I approached the sidewalk that ran around the mall, I spotted a woman in a floor length chinchilla fur coat. She looked toward the far end of the mall. I followed her gaze. Jim Insendo, the white-haired man who'd been talking to Cat at the party, headed toward her. She met him halfway and they hugged. They were about fifty feet away from the SUV. Close enough to see her face light up but out of eavesdropping range. She gestured to Catnip couple of times and they shared a laugh. He handed her a small present. She held it carefully until they parted ways then tossed it in her oversized designer handbag. A car horn sounded behind me. I pulled forward and drove to Cat's house.

Her front door was unlocked. I found her in the kitchen with a green cotton apron tied over her pregnant belly. Logan had his head buried in a bowl of cat food and Detective Madden sat in a chair by her dining room table. He wore a black suit and white shirt. Today's tie was marigold.

Floral arrangements in baskets were lined up by the back door. "What's all this?" I asked. I gestured toward the flowers, but it could be argued that the same gesture included Madden.

"They started arriving after you left. There's more but the smell turned my stomach so I put them out back." She pushed the curtain aside and I saw a row of white plants and wreathes decorating her otherwise barren patio. "This one is from Kenner & Winn. It's the nicest of the bunch so I thought I should try to keep it for the memorial service." She adjusted a leaf and then looked at me.

Madden folded his hands and leaned forward on the table. "You're a well-liked woman, Ms. Lestes. Between the casseroles and the flowers, it's obvious."

She turned on the faucet and ran her fingers under the water. "I know a lot of people through the store."

"These are from customers?" I asked.

"Customers, vendors, neighbors, extended family." she said. "It was on the afternoon news. I saw it at the doctor's office."

I looked back and forth between her and Madden again. There was no tension in the air, but the detective showed no signs of leaving. The brown mug that Cat had almost broken the night of her fit was on the table, and a used tea bag sat nestled in a spoon to the right of the mug.

Logan lifted his head from his food bowl and licked his whiskers a couple of times. He turned and looked at Madden, and then lowered his head and scurried out of the room with his tail low.

"I'm almost finished here and then you can have my undivided attention," Cat said. "You like lasagna, right, Sam?" One hand was on a rectangular glass dish that was layered with large flat noodles, ricotta cheese, tomato sauce, and something green. The noodles, cheese, and sauce were identifiable at a fifty foot distance. The green thing—a vegetable, I guessed—wasn't my area of expertise. I was pretty sure a vegetable couldn't ruin a perfectly good tray of lasagna.

"I love lasagna."

"Good. I added kale. You're okay with that, right?"

"Sure. I put kale in my lasagna all the time," I lied. "How did things go at the doctor?"

"Everything's fine. I told her about what happened and she said it's more important than ever that I meditate and try to establish a calm space." Cat slid the lasagna into the oven and set the microwave timer. "Detective Madden has been

67

keeping me company while you and Dante were at the store. Where is Dante?"

"He's still at the mall. Somebody stuck a knife in my tire and he's changing it."

Madden set down his mug. "Did you file a police report?"

"I called and they told me to fill one out online."

"You didn't catch the vandals, did you? Get a description or a lead?"

"No. Why is everybody asking me that? Usually the police want me to stay away from criminals. Now you're all asking me if I caught one."

He chuckled. "It's taking all of our manpower to respond to the calls we get so the chief determined some crimes were non-emergency. Vandalism is one. Sad to say it happens this time of year. Fill out the report online and someone will follow up with you."

"Speaking of the crime wave, how's the investigation going?" (I didn't really expect him to answer, but you can't blame me for trying.)

"It's going," he said.

"Detective Madden was telling me about the evidence they found at my store," Cat said.

"You were?" I was surprised.

"It's hard to say what was important and what wasn't, especially in a store that gets a lot of traffic this close to the holidays," he said.

"They found footprints," Cat said. "Isn't that right, detective?"

"Not sure if they're pertinent, but we did notice footprints that were deeper in the pile of the carpet than the other impressions we found, which indicates that the person might have been running. They was pointed toward the gate."

"How far apart were they?" I asked.

"The distance between the prints was also in line with the running theory."

"Anything else? What was the shape? High heel? Loafer? Sneaker? Man or woman?"

"Round toed boot. Not conclusive one way or the other, but not a very large print so I'm not ruling anybody out just yet." He took a pull on his coffee. "Ms. Lestes, you don't happen to own a gun, do you?"

Both Cat and I were surprised by the seemingly unrelated question. "Of course she doesn't own a gun," I said.

"Actually, I do," Cat said.

We both looked at her. "Let me guess. It's a pearl handled revolver," I said.

"No, it's a Ruger LC9. George bought it for me. He said I should have a way to protect myself when he was out of town."

"Where is it now?" Madden asked.

"In a case under my bed. I admit I don't like owning the thing, but George said it was necessary." She looked at me and then at Madden. "I haven't fired it since the day my brother took me to the firing range to practice."

"When was that?" Madden asked.

"Three years ago."

"Why are you asking about a gun? Are you worried for Cat's safety?" I asked.

Detective Madden looked at me but his response was aimed at Cat. "Ms. Lestes, I'm going to need to see that gun."

Cat gave Madden the gun and he left. I excused myself and showered off the crime scene. When I came out of the bathroom, Cat was in her bed. A meditational podcast played from the phone on the side table. I went downstairs and wondered what the detective knew that we didn't. By nine thirty, I was asleep with Logan curled up next to me.

11

SUNDAY MORNING

The next morning, I woke, showered again, and dressed in a white cashmere tunic, brown tights, and a brown tweed skirt. Cat was making leek pancakes and some kind of green juice.

"I can't believe you sent Dante to your house," she said. "He could have stayed here. There's room."

"Cat, I'm already sleeping on your sofa. Where was he going to sleep? The garage?"

"There are two sofas in the living room."

"I don't think that would have been a good idea."

"You don't trust yourself," she said. (Like brother, like sister?)

"I trust myself just fine."

"Have you told Nick?"

"About what? I didn't tell him about Dante and me going to your store. He has a lot on his mind and I didn't want to stress him out further."

"Sam, the man has made it clear that you're a part of his life." She put her hands on her hips and the residual of uncooked leek pancake batter flipped off the end of the spatula. "Does that scare you?"

"'Scare' isn't the right word. I've gotten used to my autonomy and for a long time it's been me making decisions about me. Reporting in to someone else doesn't come naturally."

"Calling your boyfriend to talk to him about what's going on in your life isn't 'reporting in.' It's communication."

"I know. I'm just not good at it." I sipped at my glass of green juice (the coffee wasn't ready and, frankly, I was afraid to ask what it was.)

"How come? How did you get to be your age and not know the fundamental rules of maintaining a solid relationship? You can't tell me you've never been in love."

"I was in love with Tommy, who took me to my high school prom. And Milo, the fraternity brother I dated for two years in college. And Sal from the deli counter across the street from Bentley's—no, I think I was just in love with his spicy salami."

She set the spatula down and looked at me.

"Not like that. He gave me free lunch meat."

"So?"

"So what? We didn't have all of this cell phone and social media stuff when I was in high school. Things were simpler then. You decorated somebody's locker and they asked you out."

"Yes, and when Tommy took you to the prom you had to walk uphill both ways. Come on, Sam, you're avoiding the subject. Forget high school and college and the lunch meat connection. You like Nick. You've liked him for over a decade. Now that you have him are you bored? That's what Dante thinks."

"Dante talks to you about me?"

"I probably shouldn't have brought that up, but you know what I'm saying, right?" Cat asked.

"Don't you want to talk about the investigation? Madden told us all kinds of stuff last night. That was weird, right? Why was he so forthcoming?"

"I don't want to talk about that. If you tell me the store is ready to open, I'll go in and open it."

"The store is ready to open."

"Fine. I'll call my staff and we'll pretend it's business as usual."

"That's called denial."

"No, it's called finding a way to function."

"Well, not talking about past relationships is *my* way of functioning."

Cat flipped the pancakes. "I'm not trying to pry. I know Nick's important to you. I've seen it ever since I met you. But I also know my brother. He's going to buzz around you like a fly unless you swat him away. He likes what he can't have because it's a challenge. I've watched this my whole life. I love him because he's my brother, but that doesn't mean I don't see his flaws. If you want to date them both, then date them both. There's nothing wrong with that. But you better be honest with Nick."

"I don't want to date them both! How come we're still talking about me? Your problem is a lot bigger than mine."

"I'm not sure I agree with that." She eased the leek pancakes off the griddle and laid one on each of the plates on the counter. We ate in silence. As soon as I was done, I excused myself and dug the Nick Phone out of my overnight bag. The battery was low so I plugged in the phone and left it on the counter.

It was about forty degrees outside, cold enough for a scarf and jacket, but still unseasonable warm for December. If we didn't have snowfall in a week, it wouldn't feel like Christmas. Cat drove us to her store. The gate was up and customers were milling about shopping.

A petite, scowling girl with blue hair and more than a few man-made holes in her head stood behind the case of pearls with the keys in her hand. Her pants looked synthetic and her shoes were of the Herman Munster variety. She hollered out to get Cat's attention.

"Who's she?" I asked. I felt like I'd seen her before, but wasn't sure why. Her heavy makeup and high number of piercings made her look like a lot of other goths around town. In the quest for individuality, their style had turned formulaic.

"Shana Brice. My new assistant manager. She looks a little scary but her recommendations were solid."

Empty black velvet-lined trays sat on top of the jewelry case, and clear plastic bags of jewelry sat next to them. The mauve fixtures I'd used were off to the side. I'd merchandised that case with the precision of someone with OCD rearranging a partially full container of eggs. Unless there'd been a rush on cheap pearl knockoffs in the past half hour, there'd been no reason to redo it.

Cat and I walked to the counter. "Hi, Shana," Cat said. "I didn't expect the store to be open already."

"I called the management office this morning to find out if we could get back in. They said sure, the police were done." She looked at me. "Are you new? I could use some help redoing this case."

"I don't work here. I'm Cat's friend. Samantha." I held out my hand to her. She looked at it and then kept working on the case. "What are you doing?"

She scowled at me, though I wondered if it was a natural expression or if the heavy black eyeliner and brow paint on her face created it. "I'm rearranging the merchandise. Somebody wasted this case with a bunch of cheap pearls."

73

Cat turned to me. "I thought you merchandised the cases last night?"

I nodded. I didn't want to explain my reasoning for using the inexpensive pearls instead of the more valuable inventory in front of Shana so I said nothing.

"We don't lock up the cheap stuff," Shana said. "It goes on the top-of-counter fixtures. Anything under two hundred dollars up top."

"Sam was just helping out," Cat said. "I didn't tell her our merchandising standards." She thanked Shana and turned away.

"Cat, there's mail here too," Shana said. She glanced at me quickly. "I don't know why it was on the counter and not in your office."

"That was me too," I said. I took the stack of envelopes from Shana and held them out to Cat. "The mail was on the floor at the front of the store last night, probably somebody pushed it under the gate. I didn't know where to put it so I figured it was best to put it where you'd see it."

"Good thinking. Shana, it looks like you have things under control. Sam, can you come with me to my office?"

"Sure."

As we headed through the store, the lights and the security gate by the mall entrance started to descend. I ran to it and threaded my fingers through the metal like Dante had last night. I yanked up but the gate kept moving. I reached for the control panel, hoping the switches were labeled. Not only weren't they labeled, there weren't any switches. Inside the metal box was a tangled mess of wires.

I yelled to Cat for help. She ran to the control panel and flipped a switch under the wires. The screeching of the gate subsided and, moments later, it stopped.

There was one remaining problem. The toes of my pink lizard boots were dissected underneath it.

12

Cat had a panic-stricken look on her face that was at odds with her chic red hair and elegant green dress. "Are you okay?" she asked.

Actually, I was a little shaken up. I bent down and unzipped the boots, and then pulled my feet out one by one. Fortunately for my future footwear choices, it was only the pointy tip of the boot that had been damaged, not my toes.

A customer, bundled up in an oversized gray coat, stood next to the gate. "My packages are under there. Now I'm going to be late getting my kids. I don't have time to wait while you fix this."

I looked at the packages and then at the woman. She had set multiple shopping bags on the floor while she'd stopped to sort through a display of Art Deco-inspired salt and pepper shakers.

Cat's professionalism took over. "I'll arrange to have everything delivered to you. Let me get your name and address." She looked at Shana and pantomimed writing something on a notepad. Shana ejected a length of register tape and brought it and a pen to Cat. "Your address?" Cat asked. The woman didn't answer. "Are these gifts? We'll arrange complimentary gift wrap along with the free delivery. Now, your name?"

The woman provided her name, address, telephone, and probably would have given her Social Security number and blood type if she thought Cat would throw in a few extras. Cat handled the issue gracefully, the true hallmark of customer service. When the woman was gone, Cat gave the information to Shana. "Call a delivery service and wrap these. I'll call maintenance to deal with the gate."

I followed Cat to her office. She sat behind her desk and called security. "This Catherine Lestes at Catnip. Yes, that's the store. The security gate malfunctioned. Customers are trapped inside." She paused. "Yes, I'd say this is more of an emergency than a lightbulb out in the ladies room." She slammed the phone down. "I should have kept the store closed. Did you see the crowd out there? Those people aren't shopping. They're just here to see the freak show. And lookie! Faulty gate traps people in store. We just gave the newspaper their follow up story."

"Cat, that wasn't a faulty gate. You saw the jumble of wires in the control panel. That was sabotage and you need to call the police. Dante and I checked the gate last night and it was fine."

Tears formed and fell and she swiped them away. "Damn hormones," she said. "I never cried this much before I was pregnant."

"Who has a key to the store?" I asked.

"Everybody on my staff. I want them to trust me." Neither of us mentioned the irony. "What am I supposed to do? I can't do everything myself but I can't trust anybody either."

"Cat, don't you think it's suspicious that all of this is happening now? The thefts and the vandalism? In the same week your husband was murdered?"

She went pale. I paused for a moment, expecting her to tell me to stop talking about the murder. I took her silence as encouragement to continue. "Dante and I cleaned the store last night. The gate was fine. Those envelopes," I pointed to the mail, "were under the gate. Whoever delivered it did so between the murder and the police releasing the crime scene. It's one more thing that's out of order."

She opened the top envelope, pulled out a sheet of paper, and then handed it to me. "It's the invoice for the pearls that were stolen," she said.

I scanned the page. Cat's payment terms were Net 30. It was common practice for distributors and designers to set up payment terms with existing retail accounts. "Net 30" meant that Cat was expected to pay in full thirty days from the date on the invoice.

"When did you place that order?"

"A couple of weeks ago when George first told me about the pearls."

To hear Cat tell it, George had done her a favor by cutting her a special price on his inventory, but I couldn't help wonder if he'd been motivated by something else. Breaking off a ten-year marriage the month before his wife has their first child wasn't the action of a man afraid of his future, it was that of a man who was desperate for an escape hatch. He was one of the few people who knew the full value of the inventory at Cat's store and knew exactly where she'd merchandise it. I wondered again why he was at the store the night he was killed. It was starting to look like he'd been in on the theft all along.

Cat interrupted my thoughts. "I should never have placed that order. Business as usual is an expression for a reason."

"No. The way to get ahead is to take risks, and if you wanted different results, you had to try something new. Your instincts were on target. You never could have predicted what happened."

I set the invoice down as a different idea came to me. "Didn't you tell me you bought workrf here before you owned the place?"

"Yes, from Jim Insendo. You met him at the holiday party, remember?"

"Why'd he sell?"

"He hit a point where it wasn't fun for him anymore. He wanted to have time to travel. He sold the store to me in a turn-key transaction"

"Why was he at the holiday party?"

"He was in business for a long time, and sometimes he consults for companies."

"But you said you never ordered from Kenner & Winn."

"Jim did, but I didn't. When I bought Catnip, I took over the store with the inventory as it was, but as we sold out of his inventory, I found new resources. That's been my favorite part of owning a boutique. Why so curious about him?"

"No reason."

I hadn't given much thought to seeing Jim on the sidewalk outside of the store. He could have been shopping or visiting friends at the outlets. And I could already tell Cat wasn't the type to sit around and theorize about the murder, but too many seemingly random things were happening for me to ignore them. I would have liked to call Eddie, but the needs of the visual department had kept him busier than Santa's elves.

Cat pushed the invoice back into the envelope and set it in her inbox. We left her office and she pulled the door shut behind her. Two men in brown coveralls worked on the gate by the mall entrance. Shana directed customers to the door that exited onto the sidewalk. Cat joined the workers and I wandered down the aisle. Until Dante showed up with my keys, I was stuck in the store.

Thanks to Tradava I had both money and time to burn, a rare new circumstance. Add in the fact that I hadn't even started my holiday shopping, and the decision to hang out at Catnip was a no-brainer.

I idled by a table of cashmere sweaters and considered how wrong it would be to shop for myself and not the many people on my list. Just as I was about to continue on to the men's department, I got distracted, but not by merchandise.

The woman who I'd seen outside the mall last night with Jim walked into Cat's store. She was wearing the chinchilla coat. She shrugged out of the coat, revealing a beige crocodile blazer underneath. I quickly found Cat arranging and pointed the woman out. "See that woman? She was hanging around your store last night after Dante and I left."

"Which woman?"

"That one. Right there. In the beige crocodile jacket."

Her eyes grew big. "I don't see anyone other than Lela."

"Who's Lela?"

She pointed directly at the blonde. "Lela Sexton. My top associate."

13

I looked at the blonde again. "How come I don't know her?" I asked. "I shop here all the time."

"She worked here when I first bought the store, but one of those big luxury stores in King of Prussia recruited her and she left. Now she's back and the timing couldn't be better. Remember I said somebody quit the other day? Lela called and asked if I had any openings. She's not management material but knows how to sell and she buys enough to keep the lights on."

If Cat wasn't going to wonder why her associate was sneaking around the mall after dark, then I was. Cat went back to her office and I approached the jewelry counter. I pasted on what I hoped was a friendly smile. "Nice jacket."

"Thank you. It's one less thing to lock up at the end of the night."

I decided to play dumb. "You work for Cat? We haven't formally met. I'm a friend of hers, Samantha Kidd." I held out my hand.

"Lela Sexton." She offered up her fingertips to shake, just like Joyce Kenner had. Who shakes a hand like that? Was this a thing I hadn't read about on social media?

Lela glided toward a couple of customers that had wandered into the store. If Cat was paying her associates enough to buy crocodile blazers then maybe I was working at the wrong retailer.

I watched Lela from afar. It wasn't just the expensive jacket that made her stand out. Her taupe silk shell and matching skirt, her thick gold necklace with the single pearl pendant, her gold chain belt...it was understated elegance. Most people didn't know how to do that. And for sure most people who knew how to do that weren't looking for work in an outlet store, even with Cat as the owner.

I hid behind a display of sunglasses. As I tried on pair after pair, I fake-looked around for a mirror, while really keeping my eyes on Lela. She was at home in the store. Her keys didn't jangle around her wrist like most sales associates who work in stores that lock up their pricey merchandise, but rather hung from the end of a chain belt that she had slung around her waist. She smiled at everyone and assisted them as if she were the hostess at her own cocktail party. There was no air of retail angst in her; she made the job look like the prize in a popularity contest. I pulled on a pair of round purple frames and glanced at her feet. She was doing it all in three-inch heels.

I didn't know what I was hoping to see, but this picture of perfection never slipped up. When the customer rush subsided, she stepped out from behind the cases of jewelry and walked toward me. I unfolded a pair of silver frames and pretended to admire myself in the mirror, even though they weren't right for my face.

"The plum ones would suit you better." She handed me a pair with a three-digit price tag. "I noticed you trying to get my attention, but I couldn't get away. It's tough when it gets busy and there's no one else around. Cat needs more staff."

I thought carefully about my choice of words. "Maybe she can't find people she can trust."

She looked at me like royalty who'd been challenged by one of her subjects. "She said that?"

"No, just my theory."

Her eyes stared into the sunglasses that were perched on my face.

"You really should consider those frames. They set off your cheekbones nicely." She excused herself and walked away. She'd turned my surveillance mission into a need for high priced eyewear.

She was good.

I amassed a pair of cashmere socks (for Nick), a purple scarf (for Eddie), and seven sweaters (for me), and then, feeling guilty over my obvious one-for-you-a-whole-bunch-for-me shopping strategy, put it all back. Dante came into the store while I was rehanging the socks. As soon as he saw me, he headed my way.

"Cashmere socks. Wow, that's an intimate gift. Who's the lucky fellow?"

"My brother-in-law," I lied. I held out my hand. "My keys?"

He pulled them from his pocket. He put his left hand under mine and placed the keys into my palm with his right. He closed his right hand over the top of mine, making a hand-and-key sandwich that was not altogether appropriate. I balled up my fist around the keys and pulled my hand out.

"Do you always keep your house at a steady fifty degrees?" he asked.

"Um, no?"

"I didn't think so. Your pilot light was out. I fixed it, but still had to dig a couple of blankets out of your hall closet. Cat called me when you two left this morning and I went to her place." He pulled a cell phone out of his pocket. "Is this yours? It was charging in her kitchen. My sister is anti-Apple so I know it's not hers."

It was the Nick Phone. I took it and clutched it to my body. "Yes, it's mine. You didn't look at it, did you?"

"Why? Did you use it to take selfies in your underwear?" He pretended to try to see the screen and I blushed.

"No," I said. "Thanks for changing my tire and taking care of my house."

"No problem. Just be careful—you're driving on a donut. You'll want to get a real tire on that car soon."

I left Catnip and drove home. It was early, but I was tired. I had every intention of taking a bath, putting on my pajamas, filing the vandalism report, and crawling into bed.

Plans can change.

The door pushed open when I stuck my key into the lock. The living room was dark but lights were flickering in the kitchen. I stood still, listening for unusual sounds. The house was eerily silent. And then, footsteps. Coming down the stairs.

I ducked into the coat closet and pulled the door shut behind me, wondering if the perpetrator was aware of my presence. My heart pounded in my chest so loud I was certain it could be heard down the block. The vacuum cleaner handle caught on the hem of my skirt and then slid underneath it.

The footsteps stopped. I'd spend the next twenty-four hours in the closet if it was necessary, but sooner or later I was going to have to get out of there. The front door was only a few feet away, and if I was lucky I could make it to my car and drive away before my intruder could get to me.

The vacuum cleaner handle was cold against my tights. I shifted my weight and stepped on the hem of a trench coat. The coat fell from the hanger. The hangers knocked against each other in a symphony of wood and metal. Whoever was outside the closet had to have heard.

I unsnapped the vacuum cleaner extension and aimed the angled end like a weapon. Shadows formed below the door. It was just a matter of time until I was exposed.

14

SUNDAY AFTERNOON

"Kidd, are you going to come out anytime soon or do I have to refrigerate dinner?" Nick's voice asked.

I opened the door and stared at him. "You're back? You're here? How is it that you're here?"

"I persuaded the factory owner to show up early and caught the red-eye. Surprise." He had one hand on either side of the door frame. The sleeves of his taupe sweater stretched across his shoulders and chest, and hinted at muscles underneath the argyle pattern. His dark curly brown hair was mussed up in a way that suggested he'd slept on it, and he had a two day beard growth. But it was his eyes, his root-beer-barrel colored eyes that got to me the most. They searched my face, crinkling at the corners with the faintest hint of a smile when he took in the vacuum cleaner attachment weapon. He leaned down and kissed me. "I missed you."

He'd spent his night on a red-eye so he could be with me. He had come straight here from the airport. He was standing in front of me, in the flesh. Not in Italy. Not with Amanda. And had he just said something about dinner?

"Not that it's not entertaining to watch you converse with the voices inside your head, but can you give me an indication of how long that's going to last? I need to figure out if the chicken parmigiana is going to burn."

"You seriously cooked dinner?"

"I seriously cooked dinner. Take off your coat, put away the weapon, and join me for a glass of wine."

I did as told, though not because I was good at taking directions. I was shaking and only some of it came from the terror in the closet. I'd seen Nick in a tuxedo and in jeans and he looked good either way. Today he was rumpled and he wore that well, too, like Indiana Jones in Italian adventure clothes.

I tossed both the coat and the vacuum attachment onto the sofa, gave him a quick smile, and went upstairs to my bedroom. It wasn't until after I returned, comfy in jeans, silk shirt, and cashmere socks that I joined him in the kitchen. There were a lot of questions I wanted to ask, and only a few of them had to do with dinner. Most of them ran along the why-are-you-home-so-soon? and did-Amanda-come-home-with-you? variety.

Dinner, I was happy to discover, wasn't just a box of pasta and a jar of readymade sauce. Instead, I was greeted with two plates of appetizers: melon wrapped in prosciutto and fresh sliced tomatoes and buffalo mozzarella garnished with basil and drizzled in olive oil.

"Is all of this really in season?"

"Do you really care?"

Good point.

I opened a bottle of wine while he tended to the deliciously smelling entrée.

"You're game for Chicken Parmigiana, right?"

Secret rejoicing—except, "Did you put any green vegetables in it?"

"Why would I put green vegetables in chicken parm?"

"Never mind." A few minutes went by while I sipped my wine.

Nick moved around my kitchen as if he'd done it a hundred times. "I have to admit, I'm a little disappointed in your reaction."

"To what, dinner? I'm totally impressed." I'm not that stupid. I knew exactly what he was referring to.

"To my being in your house."

"I've been trying to figure out a good way to broach that subject."

Just then, the Nick Phone rang. Being that Nick was the only one who knew the number, I didn't answer. Nick picked up the phone and glanced at the display. He didn't move for a moment. He set the phone down.

I picked up the phone and turned it toward me. The missed call had come from "Hot Man." I switched the ringer to off. "Telemarketer," I said.

"Sure." Nick stood up and checked on the chicken.

I grabbed the phone and went to the living room. I pressed the message replay button and held the phone to my head. "Sam, it's Cat." I relaxed ever so slightly. I couldn't explain "Hot Man," but I could explain Cat calling me. "I'm still at the store." Papers rustled in the background. "Call me back. Okay? Soon."

I poked my head into the kitchen. "I need to check on Cat. It'll only take me a minute."

Nick nodded his head but didn't look at me.

I called her at Catnip. "It's Samantha," I said.

"I tried to call you at my house but you weren't there. Where are you? And how come Dante has your new number and I don't?"

"I'm at home. I was going to get a change of clothes but Nick surprised me."

"I thought Nick was in Italy."

"That was the surprise. He's here. He was here when I got here."

"Then where's Dante?"

"How should I know?"

"He said he left something at your place. I thought he'd be there by now."

I froze. If what Cat was saying was true, there was a very good possibility that Dante was either on his way over or was already in the house.

I looked over my shoulder. No Nick. I crossed the room and poked my head into the kitchen. He was bent over the oven peeking inside. "Everything okay in here?" I asked.

"Yep. We have about half an hour until it's done." He closed the oven and came over to me. I held the phone face-in toward my shoulder. He put his arms around my waist and smiled. "I was thinking about taking a shower to freshen up before dinner."

"Good idea," I said. "I mean, sure, go ahead. You know where it is."

He moved his right hand up toward my face and cupped my chin. "Do you want to join me?"

Before I could answer him, I realized that the tinny sound I heard was Cat's voice coming from the phone. I stepped backward and held up my finger, and then put the phone to my head. "Cat, I gotta go."

I fumbled with the screen until I found the End Call button, and then set the phone (face down) on the counter behind me.

"You go ahead," I said. "I, um, wasn't expecting company and my bedroom is a mess. Not that we're going to be in the bedroom, but I should make sure there aren't any panties lying around. Not that I throw my panties around. I mean—"

Nick pressed his finger to my lips. "The clock is ticking. I'll shower in the hall bathroom." He removed his finger and leaned down and kissed me. I temporarily forgot about the Dante problem.

The Dante Problem!

Dante had spent the night and now he was on his way over to get something he'd forgotten. There had been no evidence of Dante in my living room or kitchen. What did he leave behind? And where was it?

I waited as patiently as I could (not very) until I heard the sound of running water coming from the bathroom at the top of the second floor landing. I crept up the first two stairs, and then a hand clamped over my mouth from behind. A second arm circled my waist and lifted me from the stairs, pulling me backward.

15

SUNDAY EVENING

The strong arm around my waist pivoted and set me down on my living room floor. I spun around and looked at Dante. His hand was still over my mouth. He leaned close and the scent of cinnamon came off his breath.

"If you don't want Loverboy to find out I'm here, you better be quiet."

I grabbed his hand and pulled it away. "How did you get in here?"

"I came in through your garage. I've been on the other side of that door for the past ten minutes."

"Then you heard..."

"Yep." He grinned. "I was hoping to hear more."

I glared at him. "What did you forget?"

"My leather jacket."

"I've never once seen you without your leather jacket."

He shrugged. "Must be Freudian. You know, like my subconscious wanted an excuse to come back here."

"Where is it?"

"In your bedroom."

"You slept in my bed?"

"I told you it was cold. I thought being in your bed might warm me up."

"You have to leave. Now."

"I'll leave as soon as I get my jacket." He started up the stairs and I grabbed his arm.

"No way, José. You go out front. I'll get your jacket." I yanked him backward (he barely budged), and charged up the stairs two at a time. His leather jacket was folded neatly on top of my pillow.

Forgot, my ass.

I pulled a pillow out of its case and stuffed the jacket inside and then threw it over my shoulder like Santa Claus. The water in the shower turned off. I ran downstairs and looked for Dante. He wasn't there. I opened the front door and was hit with a blast of cool air. Cat's car was parked in front of Nora's house next door.

Great. Dante had disappeared and I had his (recognizable) leather jacket in a pillow case in my house. Like that was going to be easy to explain. I tossed the pillow case out the front door and it landed in the bushes by the front porch. I shut the door just as Nick came down the stairs. His hair was wet and he rubbed a towel against the side of his head.

"It's cold down here," he said.

"The pilot light keeps going off. I should check it. You wait here." I ran past him and down the stairs to the cellar.

Dante stood at the bottom of the stairs. His arms were crossed over his chest. He raised both eyebrows. "My jacket?"

"It's out front in the bushes. In a pillow case." He stood watching me, not moving, not reacting. "I had to think fast.

Nick finished with his shower and I didn't want him to find you here."

"Why not? Nothing happened. Nothing's happening. This..." he dropped his arms and moved away from the closet door "...is completely innocent. Right?" He gestured back and forth between us and walked straight toward me.

I put my hand palm-side out. "Right. But still, you have to leave. Go out the garage door and be stealthy. And call your sister. She's looking for you."

I returned to the kitchen. Nick had changed into a gray turtleneck sweater and brown slacks. His face was clean-shaven. He opened the oven and pulled out a clear Pyrex dish that immediate filled the room with the scent of tangy tomato, melted mozzarella cheese, and chicken. I temporarily lost track of everything in my life and closed my eyes, inhaling the scent. I could get used to this.

An hour, half a bottle of wine, and the most spectacular dinner that had ever come from my kitchen later, I moved my napkin from my lap and set it next to my empty plate.

"You have a choice. Coffee or ice cream," I said.

"You have room left for ice cream?"

"I always have room for ice cream." I smiled. "But, point taken. Coffee, it is."

Nick excused himself. As soon as he was out of the room, I grabbed my old phone and the Nick Phone and worked on syncing my contacts. One of these days I'd delete the numbers I no longer needed, but then again, you never know when you'll be driving through New Jersey and want to call ahead to your favorite pizza joint to place an order. When the process was finished I called Cat.

"Hi," she said. "The store's really busy so I can't stay on the phone for too long. It's like what happened gave me free publicity. Everybody wants to shop at the crazy lady's store."

"Nobody thinks you're crazy."

"*I* think I'm crazy. Why wouldn't they?"

It was hard to argue with logic like that. "Listen, about tonight, I think I'm going to stay here," I said.

"I figured as much, what with Nick coming home. Enjoy your time together. This is my problem, not yours." She paused. "Maybe I'll stay at the store overnight."

"Cat, I don't think you should be pulling an all-nighter at the mall. What about Dante? His night should be wide open."

"He said he had plans."

"Trust me. His plans fell through. You are going to stay home and get a good night's sleep in your own bed. You owe it to little Andy or—"

"Don't finish that sentence."

"You owe it to your baby. And Logan's at your house. He's very good at keeping people company."

"So you're going to stay home with Nick tonight and we're just going to cross our fingers that the store will be okay?"

"Actually, I have something different in mind." I hung up and poured two cups of coffee and turned around. Nick stood on the other side of the counter.

"Is that decaf?" he asked.

"No."

"It's late. Coffee will keep us both awake. Not that I mind, but the time change is going to catch up with me sooner or later."

I handed him a mug. "Let's hope for later. I just volunteered us for overnight surveillance."

"'Overnight surveillance'? Sounds like fun."

"At the mall."

"You actually mean overnight surveillance? The mall has security guards and cameras for that."

"Yes, but we don't know if we can trust the security guards and the cameras are on the opposite side of Cat's store."

"You're serious."

"I'm serious." I ran my fingertips over his forearm. "I'll make it worth your while..."

He grinned. "I'm afraid to ask how."

Nick had, at times, opposed my involvement with the criminal element. He'd helped me out of one jam, fought with me over another. We'd broken up over it and gotten back together because of it. His agreeable nature tonight was only mildly suspicious.

It didn't really matter, though; one way or the other, the night would be fruitful. My late night investigation might turn up some new details for Cat, and I'd get to spend the night with Nick. Bonus points: because we'd be out of the house, he wouldn't discover that Dante had slept in my bed last night.

All in all, it was a win-win.

16

Twenty minutes later Nick and I sat in the cab of his truck watching both customers and employees trickling out of the outlet center. We parked on the side where Cat would have exited; there was no reason for that other than it was the most familiar to me. If something happened on the backside of the building we would need a second night of investigation.

Overnight surveillance was serious business. Before we left I changed from my jeans and silk blouse into a black cowl neck sweater, pink camo pants, and heavy black boots. So far Nick was being a trooper. My handbag did contain a Swiss army knife and an odd assortment of gadgets that I carried for potential emergencies just like this one so I still felt adequately prepared.

"Bring me up to speed on this investigation," he said.

I couldn't tell if he was taking me seriously or not, but filled him in on the highlights of the problem anyway: the smash and grab, Cat's argument with George at the party, the

95

burglar in the store, and George's body behind the jewelry case.

"If this was all about the jewelry theft, then why kill George? He left her earlier that night. Was he involved with someone else? Was this a crime of passion? But then was the smash and grab an odd case of timing?"

"You really love this, don't you?" Nick asked. "Not what happened, but this part. The questions and the evidence and the search for answers and justice."

"Doesn't everybody?"

"No. I can safely say that most women your age would not be sitting in the front seat of a truck conducting overnight surveillance on an outlet mall in forty-degree weather the week before Christmas."

"I guess that makes me unique."

"You're telling me." He reached across my lap and pulled a small black case out of the glove box. He waved his hands up and down the case like a magician prepping for a magic trick and then extracted a pair of binoculars from the case and handed them to me.

"Do you always drive around with binoculars in your glove box?"

"Only since I started dating you."

I held the binoculars up to my eyes. After a few seconds, I dropped them back to my lap. "Forty degrees?"

"Somewhere around there."

"You didn't happen to pack any blankets too, did you?"

"When I planned to surprise you, I changed into clean clothes at the airport. I picked up the ingredients for dinner on the way to your house. I didn't want to be presumptuous about what might happen after that—although if anything happened, I figured your house would have the necessary accoutrements."

"So no blankets."

"Next time I'll be more prepared."

I checked the clock on the dash. The camping store was still open, and if the temperature dropped at a rate of two degrees an hour then by midnight it would be...I looked away from the clock. I'd never gotten the hang of those "two trains leave the station at the same time" math problems and this calculation was on par with that.

I turned to Nick to see if he'd been watching. But despite sharing almost a full pot of coffee, Nick was asleep. His head was nestled between the window and the side of his head rest. His arms were around his body. The cab of the truck was cool and, with no engine running, getting colder every second. I took off my coat and tucked it in around him. His eyes opened halfway and he made a sound that I interpreted as "thank you."

Jetlag may have driven Nick to doze off in the cab of the truck, but no coat, half a pot of coffee, and the responsibilities of a surveillance had left me wide awake.

It was nine-thirty. I had about half an hour before the mall closed for the night. Half an hour to get to the camping store next to Cat's to buy a blanket (and look for suspicious activity, because as far as cover stories went, the blanket ruse was pretty solid.)

I hopped out of the truck and jogged through the parking lot toward the entrance. If we needed a flashlight, flare, or any other emergency items I would be sure to find an assortment in the camping store as well.

I asked a grungy looking clerk for the location of the blankets and was sent to the back corner of the store. Still shivering from my walk through the parking lot, I added a propane heater to the pile, along with a thermos, flashlight, and a couple of pink metallic D-clamps. They seemed like the kind of thing I should have on hand in case of emergency.

I headed toward the register. The same Hipster Hunter was working. I stacked my items on the counter and held out my credit card.

"Is there any place around here where I can get some hot chocolate?" I asked.

"There's a chocolate stand by the department store at the end of the mall, but the cups are kiddie sized."

"I mean for the thermos."

"Oh. Head out the exit and turn right. Go past the novelty sock shop and turn left. They have hot chocolate at the coffee shop, but you better hurry. It's closing time and nobody likes staying after hours."

When my shopping was complete, Hipster Hunter walked me to the door and pointed down the mall. He handed my bags to me and pulled the metal gate into place as soon as I left. I draped the handles of the shopping bags over my arms and walked as fast as I could considering I was now prepared for a polar expedition.

The hot chocolate stand was closed by the time I reached it. I cursed to myself. I left through the mall exit and was about to cut through the parking lot to Nick's truck when I saw Aguilar, the rotund security officer who'd checked on Catnip the night we found George's body, loitering on the sidewalk outside of Catnip not fifty feet away from me. I dropped down and hid behind the end of a public bench, squinting through the darkness at him.

Aguilar's presence should have been calming. Nick and I were there to keep an eye on the store, and apparently we weren't the only ones with that idea. I should have felt better knowing mall security had taken an interest in protecting Catnip, but something about the officer had felt off from the first moment he'd come to check up on the store after we'd interrupted the burglary in progress.

His hands were in the pockets of his jacket, and he looked from the bottom left corner of the door frame, up to the top left corner, across the top and then back down the right-hand side. He stepped past the door and peered into the bushes. A truck lumbered past. Aguilar lit a cigarette and sat down on a bench not unlike the one I hid behind.

It could be he was just doing his job, keeping an eye out on a store that was involved in a recent crime. Or—

The door to Cat's store swung open and a woman came out. She locked the door behind her and then headed to Aguilar. I recognized the blue-black dyed hair and the shine on her pleather pants immediately. An oversized black leather jacket with the collar turned up hid most of her face, but that didn't stop me from making an identity. I was looking at Shana Brice, Cat's assistant manager with the crappy attitude and the Herman Munster shoes.

As I watched, she set a shopping bag by her feet and locked the door to Catnip. She turned back around, reached into the bag, and pulled out a brown bundle. She tossed it in the trash can and then walked along the sidewalk to the end of the mall.

When Shana vanished from view, Aguilar stood up. He put out his cigarette and then went to the trash can. He reached inside and pulled the bundle out. He stuck it inside his brown flight jacket and pulled up the zipper then jogged across the lot to a beat-up car, climbed in, and drove away.

I crossed the parking lot to Nick's truck and yanked the door open. "Did you see that?" I asked.

Nick was asleep, his head resting against his window. His right leg was stretched out along the seat. I moved his leg and tucked a blanket around his waist. His eyes opened slowly.

"Come here," he gestured with his head, and without thinking about a master plan I slid over to him. His arm wrapped around me and the next thing I knew, we were kissing.

His hands moved to my waist, and one thing led to another. The steering wheel was behind me. The windows fogged up, and even though we were parked in the lot outside of a shopping mall the week before Christmas, it felt like a private room. And because it felt like a private room, we did things that should have been done in a private room. I may have thought briefly about the placement of the Ribbon Designer Outlet security cameras, but I don't remember. Nick had been out of town for far too long and, to be honest, I was a little distracted by what he was doing with his hands.

Once our X-rated activities came to a close, I felt around the floor boards for my panties. The insanity of the holidays had officially infiltrated my world.

I snuck a look at him. He was buttoning his shirt. He held his hand out and I grabbed it and sat up. My foot had left a print in the condensation inside of his window. He didn't seem to notice. He put his fingers under my chin and raised my face so I was looking at him. "It's been eleven years since I first saw you on a street corner outside of my showroom trying on samples that fell out of the back of my truck."

"Eleven years since I saw you in your Rocky T-shirt. I thought you were a delivery man."

"I thought you were the first woman I'd seen who could pull off a bucket hat." He smiled at the memory and put his arm around me. "It might make me seem like less of a man to admit this, but that's the first time I've ever done that in a truck," he said.

"Me too."

We kissed again, which set us off toward a round two. I put my hands on Nick's chest. "Focus. We have to focus. We're here to focus," I said. I held the binoculars up to my eyes, but the windows were too fogged to see out.

Nick cracked his window. "Give it a minute. It'll clear." I nestled under his arm and stared at the mall.

I don't remember the rest of Nick and my surveillance mission. What I remember next is being shaken awake inside Nick's truck. We were parked in front of my house.

"Kidd, wake up," Nick said.

I pulled myself away from the crook of his arm and sat up on my side of the truck, blinked a few times, and ran my fingers though my hair. The clock on Nick's dashboard said five forty-seven. It was dark, but the glow of the sun peeking up from the horizon cast the neighborhood in a pinkish-orange glow that matched my favorite Instagram filter. After a few labored breaths and wide eye blinking I looked at him.

"What are we doing here?"

"You live here."

"I know that." Another labored breath. More for emphasis than anything else. "What time is it? Why aren't we inside? Why aren't we in bed?"

He raised his eyebrows.

"You know what I mean. Why aren't we on surveillance?"

"I don't know. We were in the truck, and then we...and then that's about it. I woke and you were curled up next to me under a blanket I've never seen before." He ran his hand over the red plaid blanket on his lap. "I'm hoping you can tell me?"

"You fell asleep before I could tell you. I went into the camping store for supplies." I blinked several times and thought back over what else I recalled. "The security officer was outside Cat's store."

"That's good. That means he's keeping an eye on things."

"Yes..." The details came back to me slowly. Aguilar outside Catnip. Shana exiting the store and throwing something away. Aguilar taking it out of the trash and then leaving. There was something odd about that. "You don't remember anything?"

"When I woke up, you had your elbows propped on the dashboard. You appeared to be very focused on your task. It wasn't until the binoculars dropped from your hands that I realized you fell asleep while holding them."

"I fell asleep while on surveillance?" I asked. Talk about letting yourself down.

"It was as much a surprise to me as it was to you," he said. "I had four cups of coffee on the flight home from Italy because I thought I was going to have to keep up with you." He yawned. "It's good to know you're human."

"So that's it? You didn't see anything suspicious?"

"Kidd, it was five o'clock in the morning. The most suspicious thing in that parking lot was us."

I held my hair back away from my face. "Why are we here and not inside?"

"Because I thought it set a bad relationship precedent for me to go through your handbag in search of your keys."

I pulled my bag up to my waist and dug around the interior for my keychain. It wasn't there. I tried to remember if I'd grabbed it when we left. I looked at the house and then froze. Not because of the temperature but because someone was moving around my living room.

17

MONDAY MORNING BEFORE NORMAL PEOPLE ARE AWAKE

Nick noticed the activity inside my house too. He hopped out of the truck and stepped in front of me, using his arm to keep me back. We crept the few steps necessary to get to the front door, but circumstance wasn't on our side when it came to being unseen. The door pulled open and we found six strangers in my living room adjusting lights and placing the finishing touches on a Christmas tree. Correction: five strangers and Eddie.

Eleven months of the year, Eddie was my best friend, confidant, and occasional voice of reason. During December he was more like a figment of my imagination thanks to his responsibilities at Tradava, which was just one of the reasons I thought I was being *Punk'd*.

"What's going on here?" I asked.

"I think the words you're looking for are 'thank you for decorating my house,'" Eddie said, undaunted by the rising tone of my voice. "You're so busy helping Cat that you didn't put up so much as a twinkle light, let alone a tree. My visual staff is fried and we needed an off-site project. So, voila. A new tradition."

"I grew up here. I've had more Christmases in this house than any other place I've ever lived."

"So an old tradition. Either way, you're now ready for the holidays."

Nick came out of my kitchen with a wooden tray filled with mugs of coffee. I doubted the caffeine was going to get in the way of sleep, so I took one just like everybody else. Eddie's team packed up random items that they hadn't used and left one by one, touching base with him on what time they'd get to the store and where they should start working. Nick hovered next to me, watching them make their exit. When everyone but Eddie had left, Nick handed me his empty mug and asked for a refill.

I went to the kitchen and filled the mugs to the brim, sipped a few sips from my cup and refilled it again. I was returning to consciousness, which started to become a problem when I recognized words like *keeping her away, good timing,* and *not yet.* I set the mugs down and went back to the living room in time to see Eddie pull a set of keys out of his cargo pants and set them on the Halston book that sat on my coffee table.

"You had something to do with this?" I asked Nick. "Is that why you agreed to go on surveillance with me?" My eyes went wide. "Is that why we...in the parking lot?"

"You did what in the parking lot?" Eddie asked.

"Never mind," Nick and I said in unison.

"Dude," Eddie said. "I have to go. We did Cat's house before yours. I'm on call all day. You're on your own." Eddie looked at me, at Nick, and then back at me. He shook his head and left.

"I get the 'keeping her away' and the 'good timing,' but what did he mean by 'not yet'?"

Nick crossed the room in about three strides and tipped my face up to his. Before I knew what was happening he kissed me.

At first his lips just brushed over mine, then connected. When the kiss ended he pulled away from me and ran his hands gently down my cheeks to my neck, then over my hair. His pupils were dilated, darkening his eyes. He took my hands and walked me to the sofa, and then sat down next to me.

"Kidd, I don't know what to do about you. You're in my head. You're in my shoe collection. You're not the kind of woman I want to fool around with in my truck in a parking lot outside of a mall."

"There's another type of woman you want to do that with?"

"That's not what I mean."

"Nick, I'm not going anywhere. You've seen what my life's been like since moving back to Ribbon. Our relationship is the most stable thing I have. I don't want that to change either."

"So if I were to, maybe, make things a little more permanent, you'd say yes?"

"More permanent like how?"

He let go of my left hand and reached into his jacket pocket. He pulled out a small black velvet box. Suddenly I wasn't all that tired. A burst of electricity shot from my heart out to my fingertips and my breath caught. Nick dropped my other hand and opened the box. Inside was an engagement ring with a single square cut diamond nestled against a pale pink satin interior.

"More permanent like this."

A cocktail of emotions cycled through me, excitement and nervousness and happiness and nausea. I felt my hands shake and I balled them up to stop them. After a few seconds, I looked from the ring to Nick.

"You had that with you all night?" I asked quietly.

He nodded.

"Even when we..."

He nodded.

"And you're asking me to..."

"I'm asking you to marry me, Samantha."

"You didn't call me 'Kidd.'"

"It didn't feel like a 'Kidd' moment."

I didn't know anything about my future. What I knew was that I'd moved back to Pennsylvania to live in the house where I grew up because I'd felt like my life in New York wasn't me, but the happiest I'd been during the nine years I'd spent climbing the Bentley's New York corporate ladder were the days when I worked with Nick. Ever since I'd left, I'd been searching for something, a place where I fit. That need to find something had led me into a lot of dangerous situations and even though I'd managed to come out of them alive, each time, I was left wondering what I was really looking for. I'd had career and financial security when I was in New York, but that hadn't been enough. Nick was offering me something different. An acceptance of who I was and a promise for the future. I put my hands on his forearms and leaned in to kiss him.

I saw a new emotion in his face, one I hadn't seen before. Vulnerability? Hurt? Why was I hesitating? Why hadn't I just grabbed the ring and said yes? I knew I wanted to. I'd thought about it more than once, and if he looked on the Chinese food takeout menus in the junk drawer, he'd even see that I occasionally doodled the initials "SKT" to see what my monogram might look like.

"I'm scared," I said. It came out closer to a whisper than words.

He set the ring box down on the floor and pulled me to him. I put my arms around his neck and his were around my back and we hugged closer and longer than we ever had before. I could feel my heart beating hard in my chest—or was it his?—and I realized that this was the most secure I'd felt in a very long time.

"I don't want to scare you or rush you." he said in a soft voice next to my ear. "Just know that I love you, Kidd. I love your craziness and your impulsive nature and your need to try to fix other people's problems. I love your loyalty and your style and your sense of humor. When you put yourself in dangerous situations I wish I didn't love you so much, but I do. I've been in love with you for a long time. Nothing is going to change that. You don't have to give me an answer right now."

I felt his embrace relax and I pulled away from him. He picked the black velvet ring box up from the floor and set it into the palm of my hand.

"Where did you get the ring?" I asked.

"It was my mom's."

Emotion and exhaustion overwhelmed me. "Thank you for asking me," I said.

He caught my face between his hands and held it. Our faces were close. He leaned in for a kiss that was decidedly less innocent than the others. The fear and nausea left my body and a couple of new sensations took over. I hadn't felt this with my prom date or my college boyfriend or Sal from the deli counter across the street from Bentley's. So *this* was how it felt to be in love.

My body was sending clear signals that it was ready, willing, and able, but my brain sent up a warning flare that our first time together had been in the front seat of his truck in a parking lot, and maybe going round two on my living room sofa with the curtains not quite shut wasn't a good follow-up performance. To be honest, I'm not sure the thought was that fully formed. What I was sure about was, despite a very large desire, at least one of us needed a shower and that one of us was me.

Nick didn't appear too surprised by my gentle resistance.

"Not now," I panted.

"I know you're right," he said. "But—"

"But you know I'm right."

"I thought I was the voice of reason in this operation?" he said. He stood up and tucked his shirt into his jeans. I sat up and adjusted my bra. "I'm going to head home and spend the day with my dad. Chop down a tree, buy some presents. Do the whole men-at-Christmas thing. Talk to you tomorrow?"

"Sure."

"Take your time, Kidd. It's a big decision and I want you to be as sure about this as I am."

18

MONDAY MORNING

I gave Nick a ten minute lead and took off last night's surveillance clothes (was my sweater on backward?). I showered and dressed in a taupe scoop neck sweater, brown leather leggings, and brown wedge-heeled sneakers. I transferred my wallet, phone, keys, and lip tint into a small cross body bag. I blow-dried my hair upside down and then slipped in a quilted brown leather hair band. Twice I slipped on the engagement ring and admired the way it changed the look of my hand. Okay, three times. It was my version of dragging my big toe through the water of the deep end before jumping in.

As tempting as it was to climb into bed, I needed to check on Cat and Logan. I grabbed a couple of cans of diet cat food, pulled on an ivory car coat, and left.

Like just about everything else these days, the weather was pretending to be something it wasn't. The temperature was in the 40s and would no doubt climb during the day. Trees were bare of leaves and lawns were the color of uncooked wheat pasta. Aside from the occasional light display in a neighbor's yard, it did not feel like the holidays.

I parked in Cat's driveway and, after tapping on the front door, let myself in. Logan was curled up on top of Dante's black leather jacket on the middle of the sofa and Cat was in the kitchen.

"Good morning," she said. She seemed to be in good spirits. "I'm making banana, avocado, and yogurt smoothies for breakfast. Want one?"

"I think I'll just have coffee. I didn't get a whole lot of sleep last night." I debated telling Cat about Nick's proposal and the truck incident, but it didn't feel like the right time. She had her own issues to worry about, and my news might only serve to upset her.

She pulsed the blender a few times and then turned it off. "You shouldn't have had to worry about me. It's my problem and I need to figure it out. I should never have involved you."

"Cat, you're eight months pregnant. Whether or not this happened, you would have needed my help with the store, and even if you didn't ask me I would have volunteered. You're about to become a very busy woman and I think right now you should be resting."

"I talked to the detective last night," she said.

"Where?"

"He called. He said he wanted to come over today. He said a couple of people told him about George and my fight at the party and that raised questions in his investigation."

Warning bells went off in my head. "What did you tell him?"

"I told him about everything—George's meltdown and how scared I am about having this baby." She put her hand on her belly. "He said I didn't have to talk to him if I didn't want to, but I want this to be over."

"Cat, when he said you didn't have to talk to him, did he ask you if you wanted a lawyer to be present?"

"Yes, but my lawyer was George's friend. I don't know if they know how he was feeling. I don't know if they knew this was coming."

"Um, Cat, I don't think what George's friends think of you should be your biggest concern. It sounds like Detective Madden is looking at you as the main suspect." She picked up the blender of avocado-banana-yogurt mixture and poured it into her mug. She took a sip and stood very, very still, not saying a word for upwards of a minute. "Are you okay?" I asked.

She turned to face me. Her unfocused eyes moved up my sweater until she reached my face. "No. I am definitely not okay." She grabbed the blender and dumped the contents into the sink and then tossed the empty blender in on top of it. Droplets of green goo splattered out and landed on the backsplash and on her apron. She threw her towel onto the counter and stormed out of the room.

My first instinct was to follow her. I stood up and got as far as the doorway when I stopped to think about things from Cat's point of view. In the past four days, she'd gone from being a happily married wife about to give birth to her first child and celebrate her ten year anniversary to facing life as a single mom while mourning the death of her husband. He'd left her, and then he'd *left* her. There would be no hope for a reconciliation, no explanation for his decision or for his timing. For the rest of her life, Cat would question whether George's friends knew of his dissatisfaction, whether there was something deeper at the root of his change of heart. I didn't think she was the type to let other people's opinions shape her view of herself, but it would make it hard to reach out for help from people she no longer trusted.

When I'd first moved to Ribbon and started my life over, I'd felt alone. Cat's new reality was ten times more challenging than mine had been. I'd survived my own circumstances, but I hadn't had the extra burden of a baby on the way.

And the most frustrating thing of it all, the one thing that none of us were saying because of how it would make us appear, was that Cat couldn't be mad at George anymore. Her "Men Are Rats" rant prior to the party had been her knee-jerk reaction to being left in her third trimester by a man who selfishly said he was leaving her when she needed him the most. Nobody would have questioned her anger. But they'd fought at the party at the mall, and that was the single most damning evidence against her. Who knows how many people saw her throw her drink in his face. George had brought her wrath onto him by his actions, but when he was murdered, everything changed. George became the victim, not Cat.

And we still didn't know why.

I wandered into the living room and sat down next to Logan. He looked up at me and meowed. I ran my hand over the top of his head and scratched his ears. I picked him up and carried him to the fireplace. He put his front paws over my shoulder. Again, I looked at the photos on the mantel. The last one was of Cat when she'd just started showing. She and George stood next to each other. One of his arms was around her and the other was on her tummy. The look on his face was pure joy: eyes wide, smile even wider. Cat looked at him and he looked at the camera and anybody who saw that photo would think this baby was going to be born into the best marriage ever.

I set the photo facedown and noticed something taped to the back of the frame. It was a piece of white paper wrapped around a small, lumpy object.

I should have left it alone.

We both know I didn't.

I peeled the tape away from the frame and unwrapped the object. It was a tiny gold key. A poem had been typed on the paper:

Roses are red
Violets are blue
This life has been perfect
With just me and you.

Below the poem, written in George's handwriting, was a personal note:

My Dearest Kitty-Cat, Our family grows by one! No matter what happens, you'll never be alone as long as I'm alive. There are no words to say thank you for what we have so I won't even try. Love forever and ever, George.

P. S. Look in the flue!

"What's that?" Cat asked from behind me.

I looked up suddenly and closed my hand around the key. "It's—it's—" I searched her face as what I'd just read sank in. I was never intended to see this. Cat was.

And if what I thought was correct, it changed everything. I held the paper out toward her. "You need to see this."

"I can't take any more bad news."

"It's not bad news, I promise."

She crossed the room and took the paper. Her red hair fell forward while she read it, hiding her expression. It wasn't a long note but she stared at the paper for a very long time. A large fat tear plopped onto the paper. Finally, she lowered it and looked at me. "Where did you find this?"

"It was taped to the back of the last photo on the mantel." I held out the key. "It was wrapped around this."

She took the key and turned it over in her fingers. Slowly, she crouched down and peered inside the fireplace. She reached her hand up into the flue and moved it around. Her body tensed for a moment, and then she leaned forward more and pulled something out. It was a small box wrapped in paper with little pink and blue bows printed on it.

"How did this get in there?" she asked. I didn't reply, because it seemed we both knew the answer.

"If you had started a fire, it would have been destroyed."

"It was a joke. George baby-proofed every square inch of this place and I asked him how he was going to baby-proof the fireplace. He said not to worry—that he had something special in mind for that."

She walked to the sofa and sat down, and then slowly tore the paper away from the box. Inside was a small antique jewelry box. Cat fit the key inside the lock and opened it. A tiny ballerina spun to the tinkling tune of *Love Story*. Two small boxes were inside. One had a tag that said, "Pearls for baby." The other had a tag that said, "Pearls for mother."

A mother of pearl-handled baby rattle was inside the first box. A thick strand of the most glorious pearls I'd ever seen was inside the second. A certificate of authenticity was nestled inside the box under the necklace.

Slowly Cat closed the box and looked at me. "What does this mean?" she asked. Tears streaked her face and moistened her shirt, but she didn't sob. She already knew what it meant. She just needed me to tell her.

I stooped down in front of her. "It means George wasn't a rat."

"But he said he needed space. He told me to leave him alone."

"I don't think he said that because he wanted to. I think he was trying to protect you."

"From what?"

"From whoever it was that killed him."

19

After finding the hidden present that George had left behind, there wasn't much to say. Cat let go of the emotions that had been building up inside of her and cried on my shoulder for the better part of an hour. For once, I knew to keep my mouth shut. Of all of the situations that I'd been through, this one was unprecedented.

"I can't do this," Cat said. "I can't. I can't give up my store and be a stay-at-home mom. I can't stay at the store and raise a baby. I can't let the police arrest me for my husband's murder and plan his memorial service at the same time. I don't want to give birth in a prison! And I can't let somebody get away with taking him from me and destroying the memories of my marriage."

"So don't."

She looked at me. "Don't what? Which one?"

"All of them. Any of them. Aside from the baby, that's how I feel almost every single day."

"But it's exhausting."

"I know. So don't focus on the can'ts. Focus on what you can do. Like me. I can get a job. I can take care of Logan. I can eat a salad for dinner once a month. Stuff I can control. It's not much, but it helps me deal with the other things, the things that feel impossible."

"So where do I start? Because right now it's all so overwhelming that I can barely breathe."

"You have to be the one to figure that out," I said.

"I can't."

I didn't say it out loud, but she was kinda stepping on the whole concept.

"Cat, remember back when I first moved to Ribbon, I was hired to work at Tradava and my boss was killed? And how people suspected me?"

"Yes, but you proved them wrong."

"And you know how I proved them wrong? By accident. I didn't know what I was doing. I suspected everybody. I suspected you."

"Me? Why would I kill your boss?"

"I don't remember my reasoning. I felt like the walls were closing in around me and I was going to lose everything I had and it was supposed to be a brand new life and before I even got out of the gates, it was over. I thought I was being framed. And I didn't trust anybody, and I made a lot of accusations that could hurt people. If you knew then that I told the police that maybe you killed Patrick, we probably wouldn't be friends right now."

She stared at me, either processing what I said or wondering if she could return the favor by connecting me to the murder of George with means, motive, and opportunity. Finally, she looked down at the pearls in her lap. "I never realized how you felt when that happened. I was so mean to you. You came to my store and I kicked you out. It never occurred to me that you were fighting for your life. I'm a bad person. A bad friend."

I might have let Cat believe that I didn't remember my reasoning, but the details of that time in my life were as fresh as if they'd happened yesterday. I'd gone to Cat's store because I suspected her and nobody would listen to me. I'd planned to try to catch her in a lie or an admission of guilt, to try to get evidence to take to the police. I hadn't seen her as a person who had problems of her own, only as a person who could take the heat off me with a little redirection. Neither one of us was innocent in this scenario.

"That's all in the past," I said. "Let's concentrate on what we can do to help you out now."

"Sam, tell me what to do. Please? Until this is all over, make my decisions for me. When I met you, you were a hot mess. No offense."

"None taken." (ish).

"But now you have it all. Career, relationship, friends, pet,...I think you even lost a couple of pounds recently."

If there had been any recent weight loss, it had been thanks to Cat's vegetable-at-every-meal approach to her pregnancy. And if I had anything to say about it (which it seemed as though I was about to), I was going to put a stop to that right now.

"Are you sure about this? Because if I do this, it's only going to be until George's murderer is caught and I'm only doing it if you don't question what I tell you to do."

"I've never been more sure about anything in my life." She put her hand on her pregnant belly. "Even this."

"Okay, for the foreseeable future I make your decisions for you, starting with this. Get a fresh banana."

"A banana? You never eat bananas when you're stressed."

"You're right, but I'm making *your* decisions for you, not *my* decisions for you."

"That's not what I asked you to do."

I signed. "Fine. Get a bag of pretzel shells and meet me in the living room. We're going to recap what we know and then come up with a plan."

My experience with the local police had resulted in an unexpected friendship between me and the lead homicide investigator, Detective Loncar. The last time we'd "worked" together (he'd insist on the quotes if he read this), I'd learned that his daughter had recently had a baby but his wife, unhappy with him, had kicked him out of the house and asked for a trial separation. Loncar had never liked my involvement in his cases, but we'd broken through the initial gruff detective/amateur sleuth phase.

One of the many problems with this case was that Detective Loncar wasn't around. If I could talk to him, I could gauge how serious the police were about Cat as suspect. I could offer up counter theories. He might not want to hear them, but once they were out there, he wouldn't have a choice.

I had no experience with Detective Madden prior to his arrival at Catnip the night of the murder. He was acting like the nicest guy in the world, but if he thought Cat was guilty, nice wouldn't matter. He'd talk to everybody, collect evidence, and build a case. And once he felt his case was iron-clad, he'd go to the judge for an arrest warrant.

If I looked at things the way Madden was, I saw a pregnant, hormonal wife and a dead husband. I saw pearls from said wife's store knotted across said husband's throat. I saw witnesses who could place the wife at the same party where the victim was, describe a public argument, and place her at the scene of the murder during a window of time that I couldn't account for because I was looking for my bra in a bush outside of the mall. If Madden was already asking Cat if she wanted a lawyer present, I had a feeling he'd be meeting with the judge sooner rather than later.

But with the exception of the time I'd spent creating/retrieving my garments, I'd been with Cat. I knew she couldn't have done it. Which meant:

A) Somebody else had a reason to kill George;

B) Somebody else wanted to make it look like Cat did it;

C) We had little to no time to figure out who.

Good thing I like a challenge.

"Cat, last night I saw Shana outside of your store after hours. And before you say anything, I know it was her—with her blue and black hair and her largely synthetic wardrobe, it would be hard not to recognize her."

"So she was outside my store. She worked the late shift and probably parked on that side of the mall."

"She threw something away in the trash bin outside of your exit."

"We usually put the trash by the gate in the mall for the cleaning crew, but after the gate malfunction, she might have made other arrangements."

"But remember the security officer who came into your store the night of the party? Aguilar?"

"What about him?"

"How well do you know him? He was kind of rude to us when he first came into your store after the crash. Does he always act like that?"

"I know some of the mall security guards, but not all of them. They don't like the store owners because we blame them when we're robbed, but they say we should have better loss prevention measures. I think Aguilar was new, though, because I don't remember seeing him before the night of the party. Why?"

"Last night he was outside Catnip. He took whatever Shana threw out."

"He took her trash?"

I nodded. "Normally I'd say you should talk to outlet security, but considering they're possibly involved, I'd go straight to the police."

"Is that what you would do? Call the police?"

"Do as I say, not as I do," I said. "That detective on the case—Detective Madden—call him. He's in charge of the investigation."

"But we don't have proof that anybody did anything wrong. You said yourself that we couldn't just go around accusing people without proof."

"Did I say that?" She nodded. "Tell him you have reason to believe Officer Aguilar is involved, and then tell him what I saw."

"And how do you want me to explain that you were hanging out in the parking lot outside of my store?"

"Don't mention that part. Call him and invite him over. Show him the baby rattle from the fireplace. Let's see how he reacts and figure the rest out as we go."

20

MONDAY, NOON-ISH

This was the least relaxing vacation I'd ever had. Between Cat's troubles at the outlets, an unfamiliar detective, and Dante's general Dante-ness, I was more stressed than the day I had to present end of season projections to the CEO of Bentley's. Plus Logan had fought back on the diet by eating one of Cat's casseroles that had been left out, and I was out one pair of pink lizard boots. Nick had provided the only shining spots in a week of pre-holiday chaos.

With Cat at home resting, it was left to me to keep an eye on those who were minding the store. I headed to Catnip. Shana was behind the register and Lela was close by, folding a table of sweaters. She saw me, dropped the sweater, and walked away. "I'm taking my break," she said to Shana.

She wore another of her expensive outfits. Today it was a taupe tweed skirt suit that may or may not have been Chanel, a crisp white shirt, and a belt with a gold H in the front—instantly recognizable as Hermés. It was as if she'd been given a list of luxury brands to flaunt in front of her co-workers and customers.

I'd heard of looking the part, and between the designer wardrobe I'd accumulated while working at Bentley's New York and the more recent acquisitions from my employee discount at Tradava, I had complete confidence in my own personal style. This woman made me look like my wardrobe came from a dollar store. Cat had mentioned that Lela's spending habits helped the bottom line, but that didn't mean she didn't feel entitled to extras on the side. Even the priciest items become affordable when you implement a five-finger discount.

I watched Lela leave the store and then ducked into the lingerie department.

"Excuse me, do you have these in any other colors?" a woman asked.

I recognized the voice and turned. Joyce Kenner, the wife of half of Kenner & Winn, stood next to me. She held an assortment of lace panties that were clipped to individual clear plastic hangers. Shopping for intimate apparel fell under "personal business," and from the looks of the assortment in her hand, Mrs. Kenner's business was booming.

"Mrs. Kenner," I said, "Joyce. I'm Samantha Kidd. I met you at your holiday party. I was with Cat Lestes."

She looked confused for a moment, and then recognition struck. "Oh yes, you're Catherine's partner."

"We're not partners like you think."

"I certainly hope you're not planning on breaking things off with her because of the baby," she said. "Whatever your problems are, I'm sure you can work them out."

"It's—complicated."

"Honey, doesn't matter if it's men or women. It's always complicated." The corners of her mouth turned up but the smile didn't reach her eyes.

"No, Joyce, it's not complicated like that. Cat is married. Was married. Her husband worked for your husband's company. George Stevens?" I expected her to respond to the name. At her blank look, I continued. "He was murdered a few nights ago, right here in the store. Didn't your husband tell you?"

"My husband doesn't bring details about the company home with him."

"But it's been all over the news. That and the usual retail thefts. I don't see how you could have missed it."

"I don't share society's fascination with murder and homicide. It's unseemly." She stood straighter. "About Catherine, Tom led me to believe the two of you were a couple. I didn't mean to imply anything."

I put my hand on her arm. "It's okay. Cat's going through a really hard time right now and she can use all of the support she can get. Imagine, eight months pregnant and now this."

Her eyes narrowed for a moment. "Eight months? That would mean—last April?"

"I imagine so. I never stopped to do the math."

"Poor thing," she said. She took my fingertips in her hand and squeezed. "Do let me know if there's anything I can do to help your friend out." She glanced at the assortment of panties in her grip and then, as if realizing she had no idea why she'd wanted them in the first place, handed them to me and walked away.

It struck me as odd that Joyce Kenner didn't know about the murder at the outlet. Not only had it been on the news, but George was part of the Kenner & Winn family. He'd been strangled with a necklace that had been outsourced by her husband's company. Not that I expected talk of murder to be dinner table conversation, but this seemed like the kind of thing that might transcend "pass the salt."

I returned Joyce's selections to the appropriate fixtures and headed to Cat's office so I could adjust my leggings. Once I closed the door behind me, I tugged at my waistband until the crotch was back into place. I pulled down my sweater and squeezed through the narrow space between Cat's desk and the file cabinet and dropped into her chair for a moment. I leaned back and studied the office. The ceiling consisted of pop-out, off-white cork tiles positioned on top of a gray metal frame. My old buying office at Bentley's had the same kind. It was handy for birthday parties when we needed a place to hang balloons, because while the metal frame was rigid, the cork tiles lifted easily. One party had us celebrating an engagement by dangling ring pops from the metal grid with colorful ribbons.

Happy memories of working at Bentley's had helped fade the recollection of the sixty-five hour work weeks. I remembered the office camaraderie that we had, even though the job had held its stressful moments. The close-knit team that I assembled seemed capable of rising to most challenges and having fun between the crises. Funny thing, I hadn't thought about that job in a couple of months. Now I was remembering it as though I'd been a fool to leave.

The walls of Cat's office were soft yellow. I was willing to bet that she'd been responsible for the color choice and not Jim. My eyes traveled around the office, looking at the Erté print on the wall, the mirror that hung on the back of the door, and the file cabinet propped back against the wall. Our hidden camera was positioned between a pile of books on fashion and style, and I cringed while I realized that Dante would see me hanging out after hiking up my tight pants. As long as I managed to keep my embarrassing moments less than five minutes long I had a chance to go unnoticed.

Or, I could go back through the pictures and delete the incriminating ones and nobody would be the wiser.

I stood on top of the desk and reached for the tablet. I discovered a new vantage point, one that let me see the top of the wooden cabinets that lined the wall behind Cat's desk. I stared at a small collection of crystal frames that sat off to one side and a stack of invoices held together with a large black binder clip. A cluster of awards for best sales promotion that were seriously in need of dusting. A framed sketch signed by a fashion designer with a personalized note to Cat. I picked it up and ran my hand over the glass. That was better. Then I noticed movement reflected in the glass.

I looked around, making sure I was alone. The overhead lights were all the same as they'd been when I entered. The computer screen had long ago defaulted to its screensaver, and the small desk lamp was off. I heard a scraping sound overhead and looked up.

One of the ceiling tiles was out of place. I reached up and pushed on it ever so slightly. Like every ceiling tile I'd ever seen, it lifted with minimal pressure from my fingertips. I moved my hands to the tile to the left. Same result. There was only one tile left that was within my reach, and it wasn't sitting properly on the metal grid. I gently pressed on it but it didn't budge. I applied a little more pressure, but nothing. I checked my footing, and then stood on my tiptoes and put both hands on the ceiling tile and pushed up. The tile shifted and a cascade of pearls pelted me on the head.

21

MONDAY AFTERNOON

The unexpected shower of jewelry caught me by surprise and I yelled. I swatted at strands of black pearls as they fell on me, flinging some away. I lost my balance. My right foot knocked the inbox off the desk and papers flew everywhere. I dropped to a squat and gathered up as much of the twisted and tangled jewelry that I could.

There was a knock on the door. On instinct, I stuck my left leg out and corralled the remaining jewelry from the desk and slid it across the surface in a sweeping kick like a character in a Quentin Tarantino movie. The door to the office opened and Cat's former boss, Jim Insendo, peeked inside.

"Cat?" he asked. His eyes went wide at the sight of me in a fighting crouch on top of Cat's desk. If exercise had been more of a priority in my life, I might have been able to get back up from the squat. As it was, I tipped myself to the right and slowly brought my left leg around to the front. I shifted my right leg so I was sitting on top of the desk with both legs dangling in front of me. Only slightly less suspicious in terms of things-people-do-in-the-boss's-office.

"Cat's not here," I said. "Jim, right? I'm Samantha. We met at the Kenner & Winn party."

"Samantha, that's right." He reached forward and shook my hand. He was younger than I'd originally thought. He couldn't be a day over fifty and even that was a stretch. Must be nice, getting to choose retirement a full fifteen years before the rest of the working masses.

His eyes flicked over my shoulder for the briefest of moments, but then returned to my face. "Do you know where Cat is? I brought some paperwork for her." He held a flat white envelope.

"She's at home resting, but I can take that." I held out my hand and took the envelope. He didn't hand it over right away, and for a moment we engaged in a passive tug-of-war. When he let go, I tucked it under my arm. "I'm sort of helping her out around the store."

"I thought you worked at Tradava? Isn't working here a conflict of interest?"

I studied him. His normally jovial expression was less relaxed, and in its place was one that told me Jim Insendo didn't miss very much. I didn't know what Cat had told him about me. I pushed myself off the desk and stood in front of him, making him take a step backward.

"I'm on vacation," I said, conjuring up a smile. "Cat's had a troubling time lately and I'm doing her a favor. No pay, no benefits. Just a friend helping a friend. Isn't that why you're here?"

"Something like that."

There was something about him that seemed out of place. We stood like that for a few seconds, him fidgeting with his pockets, me crossing my arms and then dropping them to my sides to look less defensive.

Jim looked behind me again, his brows slightly furrowed. "Did I hear a crash?"

I smiled. "I knocked over her inbox. Klutzy, I guess." I inched my way forward until we were standing awkwardly close together. I pretended everything was okay but was pretty sure a necklace was caught on my shoe. Jim finally stepped back, and I kicked my foot a couple of times. The necklace dislodged and flew under the desk. I kept inching forward, making Jim move back, until we were out of the office with the door shut behind me.

"I have to take care of some things for Cat, but I'll tell her you stopped by."

"Make sure she gets that," he said, pointing at the envelope.

"I will." I scanned the store, looking for someone I could trust. Shana was by the registers, but she wasn't exactly on my trustworthy list. Dante, however, stood by the front of the store next to the control panel to the gate. I raised my chin and caught his eye, and then tipped my head ever so slightly toward Cat's office. "Would you excuse me?" I said to Jim.

"Sure. I think I'll do some shopping while I'm here."

Jim walked away. I looked at Dante again. He hadn't left his post. I bypassed the cocktail dresses and headed toward the front of the store.

This time of year, the store should have been in complete disarray thanks to desperate customers who tore apart displays in order to find last-minute-gifts but that wasn't the case. Just like Cat had said, the customers who entered weren't there to shop, they were there to gawk. Between the theft and the murder, Cat was going to post a loss this season. The news had put her store on the map, but the only people wandering through were the looky loos who wanted a story to tell on Christmas morning.

I reached Dante. "When did you get here?"

"About half an hour ago. Cat said you were here and I called you but you didn't answer."

"I found something in her office. Come with me." I turned around and led the way. I didn't say anything until after we both were inside the office with the door locked behind us.

Dante turned toward me. "You got my attention," he said. He was closer than I'd anticipated. "Though I question your choice of setting." He looked from my face to the camera.

"I came in here to get something from Cat's desk. The ceiling tiles were out of place. So I climbed up on the desk and pushed on them and that fell down." I pointed to the other side of the desk at the pile of jewelry.

"'That?'" Dante put his hands knuckle-side down on the surface of Cat's desk and leaned across. He stayed like that for a few seconds.

"I'm no fancy former private investigator like you, but if I had to guess, I'd say 'that' is the jewelry somebody stole the night we found George's body. What I don't get is how somebody ran out of the store but then got it back into the ceiling in Cat's office." I picked Cat's desk phone up from the floor and checked for a dial tone.

"Who are you calling?" he asked.

"Detective Madden. This clearly relates to the case and he needs to know."

He put his hand on my wrist. "Does Cat know about this?"

"No, but she should. You need to get your camera out of here and find out how this happened."

The dial tone shifted from a steady one-note to a rapid beeping. Dante let go of my wrist and leaned too close for comfort. He reached behind my head and picked up the camera, and then stood back up. "Keep me in the loop," he said and then left.

The number to the Ribbon Police Department was almost as familiar as my own, though there were definitely times when my first instinct hadn't been to call it. I guess that hadn't been my first instinct this time either. So much for personal growth. When the desk sergeant answered, I asked for Detective Madden.

"He's out interviewing a suspect. Whatcha got?"

"This is Samantha Kidd," I said, wondering if it would ring any bells.

There was a pause on the other end of the phone. "What are you calling in reference to, Ms. Kidd?" he asked.

"I need to talk to the detective about the murder at the Ribbon Designer Outlets. I found something he should see."

"You're calling about evidence in a murder investigation?"

"Well, sort of."

"Is it or isn't it?"

"It is."

"I'll let him know. What's the best number for him to reach you at?"

That's it? "Hold on," I said. I found my handbag and fished the Nick Phone out from the depths. There was a missed call from "Hot Man." I swiped the notification away from my screen when it occurred to me that I didn't know my own phone number. There had to be a way to find out my own number from the phone but there was a faster way to get the information. I called Nick.

"Hey, Kidd," he answered.

"Hi. I don't have time to talk. What's my phone number?"

"Shouldn't you know?"

"I know my old number but not my new number and the police are on the other line—"

"The police? I'm coming over."

"I'm not at home. I'm at Catnip. I'll explain later."

"Do you have a pen?"

"Yes, tell me when you're ready." He rattled off a series of numbers. "You know my number off the top of your head?"

"It seemed important."

I smiled. The blinking light on the base of Cat's phone reminded me I had a desk sergeant on hold. "See you tomorrow."

"About tomorrow—" he started, but I cut him off.

"I gotta go." I hung up and took the desk sergeant off hold. "Hello?" I asked. "Are you still there?"

"No wonder Loncar took a vacation," he muttered. "Ready when you are."

I repeated the number for him and he repeated it back to me. After hanging up, I left the office. I locked the door behind me and looked up just in time to see Jim turn around and leave.

It seems he'd been keeping an eye on the office the entire time I'd been inside.

22

MONDAY AFTERNOON

I went to the register where Shana was refilling the shopping bags and shoved the envelope from Jim into my handbag. Today Shana wore a black pleather vest over a turtleneck and a pair of tight black jeans. A small chain dangled from a piercing in her left nostril and connected to another piercing by her eyebrow.

"When's Cat coming in?" she asked.

"She's not. I told her to take the day off and I'd watch over the store."

"Why?" she asked. "You're not part of the staff. I'm the assistant manager. If anybody should have been asked to step up and put in more hours, it should have been me."

"You're right, Shana. You do bear a certain responsibility for the store." I looked over my shoulder. "Weren't you the one who worked the night George was murdered?"

She went even more pale than her usual shade, probably making her more attractive to other goths. The blue streak in her hair stood out in stark contrast to her extra-pale skin, and dark, purplish-blue circles under her eyes became prominent. We'd been alone in the store when I came up to her, but a woman with a basket of colorful leather gloves now approached. Retail rules dictated that we press pause on our confrontation until we could take it off the selling floor.

"Excuse me," the woman said. "Is one of you Samantha Kidd?"

"That's me," I said. "Can I help you?"

"Not me, but you can help that gentleman over there." She pointed to the front of the store where Detective Madden stood. The collar was up on his long loden-green trench coat, and his red hair curled against it in the back. He held up a hand in a mock salute.

"What is he doing here?" Shana asked. If she went any more pale she'd be invisible. I was certain she was hiding something but I didn't know what.

"The detective? How do you know him?"

"Wasn't he on the news?"

"Probably. He's here because I called him," I said. "I found something that I thought he should see." I glanced down. Her hands were shaking. She balled them up and shoved them into the pockets of her vest. I looked back at her face, making no secret of the fact that I'd observed her very suspicious body language.

I met the detective at the front of the store. "Detective Madden," I said. "Thank you for meeting me here."

"I got here as soon as I could. Dispatch said you found evidence that we missed?"

"I didn't say you missed it. I found something I think is related to the case. Truthfully, I don't know what it means so I called you. It's in Cat's office."

"Lead the way."

As we walked through the store, I wondered if Cat had told him about the present George had left behind for her. The gesture told me much about their relationship, but would the detective see it the same way?

"How are you holding up?" I asked. (Just being polite.)

"I have to tell you, I wasn't happy about getting assigned to this case. The week before Christmas, nobody wants to have to investigate a murder. And this case—it's a lot. Pregnant woman left by her husband days before a major holiday." He shook his head. "It's no Hallmark movie, I can tell you that."

I was surprised by the detective's apparent interest in discussing things. "You have to admit this is a tricky case," I said.

"How so?" he asked.

"There's the burglaries and then the murder, but aside from the fact that the victim was both the store owner's spouse and the supplier of the merchandise he was strangled with, what's the motive? Add in what I'm about to show you in Cat's office and you'll see what I mean." I paused in front of the door and studied him. "Detective Loncar would have told me to mind my own business by now."

"Detective Loncar did that for your safety. I don't think that's as much of a concern in this case."

"I agree. You should be watching out for Cat, not me. Have you talked to the security guards? And the staff? And George's employers? I know you talked to Mr. Kenner but have you talked to Mr. Winn? I could try to arrange a time for everybody to come here so you can follow up with them."

"Mr. Winn is out of the country. He has travel papers and passport stamps and hotel confirmations to back that up. His alibi is sound."

"Oh."

"Ms. Kidd, I appreciate your help. I'm sure your friend appreciates your help too." He looked behind me. "But I can't help wondering if you aren't trying to help your friend out a little too much?"

"Cat didn't do anything. I was with her the whole night. Even if she did fight with her husband, she didn't have time to kill him."

"You were with her the whole night? You didn't, say, leave her alone at the party while you went to the mall bathroom? Or after the party to retrieve something from the bushes outside?"

"How do you know about that?"

"Or go to the fitting room to try on dresses while she was inside the store? That was your statement. You were in a fitting room at the time when Mr. Stevens could have been killed?"

"I was in the fitting room while somebody smashed the jewelry case and stole a bunch of Cat's jewelry."

"You're right, that is what you told me."

"Cat couldn't have done this. You don't think George would have struggled while she was strangling him? He's not the most physically fit person in the world but if he were fighting for his life, he'd be able to overpower her."

He crossed his arms. "They told me about you. The other officers. Said it was only a matter of time until you made a call to us. I thought that kind of thing only happened on TV, like in that Jessica Fletcher show. My mom loved that."

"Detective Madden, if the other officers told you about me, then they must have told you that I've helped the city, not hurt it. Detective Loncar approved my application to Citizen's Police Academy shortly after my birthday in May."

"Have you attended?"

"Not yet. I finally got a job and haven't had a lot of spare time."

He grinned. "Maybe you should thank Loncar for that too."

"I got that job on my own merits, thank you very much," I said. It occurred to me that in the short distance from the front of the store to Cat's office, our conversation had gotten derailed. "Detective, with all due respect, I think when you see what I found inside Cat's office you'll realize there's something very off about this case."

We stopped outside the closed door. He tried the knob but I'd locked it. I unlocked it and stood back, gesturing with an open palm for him to try again. He opened the door and stepped inside. I peered over his shoulder. Everything was as I'd found it: the mess of necklaces that had fallen from the ceiling now scattered on the floor behind the desk. The ceiling tile slightly out of place. The chair pushed back, away from the desk, into the bookcase behind it.

"I came in here to—well, I needed a moment alone—and I heard something coming from the ceiling."

Madden looked up. "Is that how you found it?"

"Not exactly. I climbed onto the desk and put my hands on the ceiling and the tile shifted and all of this jewelry fell out."

He stood back. "Can you show me how you did that?"

"Right now?" He nodded. I went to the side of the desk and climbed on, and then stood up. I stretched both arms up over my head and, using my fingertips on the ceiling tile, lifted it and shifted it slightly out of place. "I did this," I said, "and then all of that stuff fell on me."

"Why is it on the floor?"

"Somebody came to the office and I didn't want them to catch me, so I flung the jewelry to the desk and kicked it to the floor."

"Who?" he asked. He never looked away from my face.

"Jim Insendo. He used to own the store. And he's strong—strong enough that, unlike Cat, he could have overpowered George. Do you need me to spell his name for you?"

"Not necessary." Madden looked up at the ceiling and then at the desk and the floor, and then back at me.

I was still standing on the desk with my hands on the ceiling tile above me. "Can I get down now?"

"Sure." he said. He held his hand out to offer assistance, but I squatted and then shifted and then climbed down the same way I had the first time.

"This changes things, right? Whoever stole this stuff the night of the murder got back in here and tried to hide the evidence. They know if you follow the theft you'll likely find them, so they found a way to get the evidence back so you can't make that connection anymore."

"I suppose that is one way to look at it," he said.

"Have you narrowed down the suspect pool now that you have that footprint in the carpet? Maybe you'll find something in here. Do you want to seal the office so you can dust for fingerprints? I'll watch the door if you need to go to your car for equipment."

"There's no need for that," he said. "Ms. Kidd, I applaud your loyalty to your friends. That's what I said to the officers who told me about you. It's rare to find someone who is so willing to stand up for people she cares for."

"Thank you," I said. Despite his words, I couldn't help the ominous feeling that crept over me. "It is important for me to help my friends. Especially someone like Cat. She has enough to deal with right now. She doesn't need this."

Detective Madden leaned close to me. "I'm pretty sure you set this up to incriminate someone who works for Ms. Lestes. The jewelry in the ceiling, the surprise discovery when nobody else was around. You just demonstrated how easy it would be for you to have done it yourself. Like I said, I applaud your motivation, but that doesn't change things."

"I'm not sure I like what you're implying."

"Then I'll come right out and say it. I think maybe there was no burglary. I think you helped Ms. Lestes hide that jewelry in her ceiling to make it look like there was another crime in play. But if that's the same jewelry that you claim was stolen the other night, I'll have no reason to believe anything except that she stole it herself to cover up the evidence that she killed her husband."

"Why would she kill him?"

"Maybe she didn't want to deal with alimony and child support. As a widow, she gets sympathy and access to her husband's benefits."

"She's not like that. She wasn't sitting around plotting how to strangle her husband. Besides, how could she physically have done it?"

"Easy. George Stevens was shot. The pearls around his neck had been added after he died."

The gun. That's why he'd asked if she owned one. "But I was there. I saw him and there wasn't any blood."

"Ms. Kidd, I'm afraid the details of the murder are part of an ongoing investigation, and I can't share anything else with you."

Great. Detective Madden's Good Cop act was slipping.

23

MONDAY, EARLY EVENING

Traffic around Ribbon had been gradually thinning out over the past week. Vacations starting early, people heading out of town. Once I escaped the magnetic pull of the shopping mall, it was smooth sailing to my house.

The temperature in the house was cool. I kept my jacket on and went downstairs to check the pilot light on the furnace. My dad had a routine with the appliances in the house. Put the instructions in a Ziploc bag and tuck them into some nook or cranny close by. This way, in case of emergency, anyone could have access to the original operating manuals. Besides, in the case of a house with a previous basement flooding problem, the Ziploc baggie protected the instructions against the elements. I felt around the front and side of the furnace until I found the yellowed plastic package and quickly scanned the directions to learn what I needed to do.

A set of hinged metal doors were hidden on the lower left of the furnace. Inside I saw a small piece of pipe—no larger than the width of a cigarette—that the instruction manual identified as the pilot light. Apparently, this was supposed to be throwing off a blue flame. I wasn't brave enough to stick my fingers underneath for confirmation, but there certainly wasn't a blue flame, or anything else, coming from that little piece of pipe.

I consulted the instruction manual again, wondering how exactly I was supposed to go about lighting anything without burning my fingers or potentially setting the room on fire. Their drawing suggested that I was to use a super long match. Now, where exactly was I supposed to find one of them?

A couple of expletives later, I found a small matchbook, a long stick, and a fire extinguisher. There was probably a better method than the one I was about to embark on, but I'd played the scenario out in my head and it seemed like this would work. A quick look at the heavens, or ceiling as the case may be, a short request for the help of St. Jude, patron saint of impossible situations, and I implemented my plan.

I talked to St. Jude a lot.

One more review of the plan. Light the match. Light the stick. Light the pilot light. Blow out the flame on the stick. Use fire extinguisher if necessary.

Now: action.

Match lit, check.

Stick lit, check.

Pilot light lit, check.

Flame blown out, check.

Of course, I forgot to turn the opposite way when I blew out the fire on the stick so I blew out the pilot light too.

Second attempt.

Match lit, check.

Stick lit, check.

Pilot light lit, check.

Turn around to blow out the stick.

Drop the stick when I see Dante leaning against the door watching me.

OOPS! Now I need the fire extinguisher!

While I fumbled to remove the pin he crossed the room and stamped down on the flame. It hadn't had a chance to do anything but burn further down the shaft of the stick since it had landed on the exposed concrete floor.

"How long have you been standing there?" I demanded.

"Long enough." He stepped closer to me, took the matches, and lit the pilot light. "I think you'll be surprised with what I found on the computer tablet."

"You found something? Good. Because we have a new problem." I told him about Detective Madden's reaction to the pearls in the office. "He seems to think that Cat and I lied about the burglary, and if we lied about that, then what else did we lie about? And he's tricking Cat into thinking he's a nice guy but if he arrests her he is definitely *not* a nice guy. Not."

"Come with me." He headed up the stairs and I followed. When we reached the kitchen, he turned and went up the next flight of stairs and turned left toward my spare bedroom. "I set up a second camera on top of the cabinet behind the desk. It picked up the file cabinet where the original camera was, plus the door and a little of the desk area. You want to see what I found? Other than the shot of you disrupting our surveillance."

"It was an accident."

He picked up a photo that showed me looking directly into the camera with my hands on either side of it. The angle made my hands look like those of a giant.

"I needed a moment of privacy."

"It's private here," he said playfully.

I felt myself stiffen. It was the same feeling I'd had from the first time I'd met Dante, only different. Him as cat, me as mouse. The nervousness, the unsettled feeling, the sense that he'd gotten under my skin when I least expected it.

"How did you program your number into my phone?"

"Okay, we're switching gears."

"My cell phone. When I left it at Cat's house there was one number in it. You brought it to me and there were two. How'd you do that?"

He smiled, and then, realizing that I actually wanted an answer, crossed his arms. "I found an unlock code on the internet. It was a joke."

"I know. But what's the deal with us, Dante? You show up here when it's convenient for you. You don't keep in touch and you say it's because I didn't call you. How come you never call me?"

"You're in a relationship."

"If that fact meant anything to you, you wouldn't have programmed 'Hot Man' into my phone. Face it, you're a loner. You want to show up, crash the party, get what you can, and then vanish. Nothing's real."

"You think nothing in my life is real?"

"How would I know? You dole out information about your life like you're dealing a hand of poker with a marked deck. You let me know what you want me to know." Being around Dante felt unstable—like how I'd felt so many times while trying to get my footing on this new life. Trying to find my place in the world. I'd cycled through being a person who knew how to handle things in New York to a person who could barely keep it together in Ribbon. Holding Cat's hand through her ordeal had reminded me what it was like when I knew who I was.

"How many new friends have you made since moving back to Ribbon?" Dante asked. "Do you know your neighbors? Have you been to a town hall meeting or gotten involved in any local events? When's the last time you saw your family?"

He studied me for a second. "If one of us is a loner, it's you. I'm going to let you sort out the photos while I check on my sister. Don't make any rash decisions, Samantha."

"What do you mean by that?"

"It means I serve a purpose in your life and we both know it." He put his hand around the back of my neck and pulled me toward him, crushing my lips with a long, hot kiss.

I pulled away. This wasn't the first time Dante and I had kissed, but if I said yes to Nick, then it would be the last. My pulse raced and I had trouble keeping my balance.

Dante left the room and went down stairs. I stayed behind and swiped through the pictures on the tablet, not able to concentrate. I set the tablet on the desk and followed him downstairs. Dante opened the front door. The Nick Phone rang in the background.

"Let me know if you find anything," he said, and left.

I went to the kitchen and grabbed the phone from the charger. It was Cat's store. "Hey, sorry. What's up?" I said. There was silence. "Hello?" I was about to hang up and call her back when her strained voice spoke.

"Are you with Dante?"

"No, he just left. I'm at home."

"Can you get to the store as soon as possible?"

My blood went ice cold despite the warmth of the newly ignited furnace. "Is everything okay?"

"Not exactly," she said. Her voice wavered. "There's been another murder."

24

"Who—where—when?" I asked.

"Aguilar. He was in my office—in my chair," Cat said. Her voice shook.

"How did he get into your office without you knowing?"

"I don't know, Sam, but the police are here and they have questions that I can't answer. Detective Madden said he wanted to talk to you. Can you get here too?"

"I'll be there in twenty minutes."

Police cars and an ambulance were parked willy nilly by the curb outside of Catnip. Lights swirled and uniformed professionals moved about. A crowd of onlookers had formed on the sidewalk, but police kept them from seeing much. It was safe to say that Cat wasn't going to be doing any more holiday business today.

Detective Madden stood outside of the store on the sidewalk with Cat. Today's necktie was light blue. Cat had a thick blanket wrapped around her shoulders and her makeup was gone. I parked and approached them.

"Sam," Cat said. She dropped the blanket and threw her arms around me. I felt her shoulders shake. I looked at the detective. He nodded at me.

"What happened?" I asked. "I thought you were going to stay at home and relax."

"I had to get out. I kept staring at the package that you found in the fireplace and thinking about George, about why he told me he was leaving me. It didn't make sense. I kept sitting there, trying to make it work in my mind but I couldn't. And I knew you were with Dante, so I came here. I thought maybe I could work on something to take my mind off things."

I bent down and plucked the blanket from the ground and then held it around Cat's shoulders. "Can we go inside?" I looked at Madden. "I think she should be sitting down."

"She wanted fresh air," he said.

"Sam, it was horrible. I went to my office to work on next month's schedule and he was just sitting there in my chair. His face was puffy and red and there were pearls tied around his throat, just like George."

"But the pearls—" I looked at Madden. "I thought you collected them as evidence when I found them earlier."

Cat looked back and forth between our faces. I'd called Dante to come and get the camera, and I'd called Detective Madden. None of us had thought to tell Cat about the merchandise showing up or what the detective implied when I told him. I honestly couldn't tell if that was a good thing or a bad thing.

"The necklace around his neck was from the Kenner & Winn shipment," she said. "It was a long strand of black pearls. The ones you asked me to hold for you."

"How do you know?"

"The hold tag was still attached to it."

A unformed officer poked his head out of the store and called the detective over. He excused himself and walked just slightly out of earshot.

"Sam, why is this happening? What did I do?" Cat said.

"Shhh. Did you talk to Dante?"

"Not recently. Why?"

"Okay, I have to talk fast. When I came to the store today, I went into your office and one of the ceiling tiles was out of place. I moved it and a whole bunch of pearl jewelry fell on top of me. I called Dante. He took the cameras and I called Madden."

She looked relieved. "So my merchandise was returned? That's a little bit of good news, isn't it? When all of this is done I have a chance to make up the sales, at least." Her brows pulled together and she looked confused. "But where did you put the jewelry? Lela didn't say anything about it when I came in."

"Lela wasn't here. Shana was. But I don't know if she knows because I only told Detective Madden. He said—he thinks—he made it sound like I could have put the jewelry in the ceiling to make you look innocent. He thinks there was no smash and grab the night we found George and that this merchandise showing up was just a way to corroborate that story to make you look like a victim."

"But I wouldn't do that!"

"I know. Everybody who knows you knows you wouldn't do that. There's only one problem."

"What's that?"

"Detective Madden doesn't know you."

An EMT pushed a lumpy white gurney out of the store, and the officer asked Cat if she thought she could make a positive ID. I squeezed her hand in an attempt to give her strength and stood close to her while they pulled the sheet back.

146

Despite the tourniquet of shiny black pearls knotted tightly around his throat, there was no doubt that we were looking at Officer Aguilar. I looked away from his glassy eyes and focused on his nametag, still clipped to his security guard uniform.

Cat stared at his face for a few seconds, and then her small hands balled up into fists. She turned to Detective Madden. "You think I did this? Really? I'm a small, pregnant woman. How would I strangle him and get him into my office without anybody seeing? How would I strangle someone who knows me and then get his body behind a jewelry case? Can't you reenact the crime and see that it's impossible?" The blanket dropped from Cat's shoulders a second time. "Follow me," she said. "I want to show you something."

She went into her store and headed to the jewelry counters. Madden followed her and I followed Madden. When she reached the aisle between the jewelry department and the shoe department, she turned to face him. "You're about George's size." She reached up for his throat, but her pregnant belly kept her from being able to reach his neck. "How exactly would this work? Oh, wait—I lassoed him, right?" She yanked a necklace from a top of counter fixture and held it taut between her hands. "How did I do it? Like this?" She stood on her tiptoes and pressed the pearls into his throat.

Detective Madden's eyes widened. He put his hands on her wrists and lowered them away from him. Two uniformed officers came over and stood on either side of her. Madden looked at them and shook his head slightly.

"Cat," I said in a low voice. "Give me the pearls."

As if coming out of a temporary fog, her expression changed from anger to fear. She looked at the pearls in her hands and at the faces of the officers around her. She dropped the necklace to the floor. Customers collected by the mall entrance watching the show.

"Nothing to see here, folks," I said. Madden and I shared a long look. "Detective, is there someplace we can talk?"

One of the uniformed officers led Cat to a nearby ottoman. Madden picked up a briefcase and pulled out a clipboard. He read something on it and then looked up. "You'd like to add something to your statement?" he asked.

"Last night I saw Mr. Aguilar come out of the mall and loiter outside of Catnip after hours."

"That's his job," he said.

"That's what I thought, too, but he acted funny. He looked around the door to Catnip and in the bushes next to the employee entrance. Eventually he sat on the park bench and Shana Brice—Cat's assistant manager—came out of the store and threw something away. Aguilar took it."

"Do you know what it was?"

"If I knew what it was, I wouldn't be so cryptic. It was dark and I was cold."

"What were you doing in the parking lot after hours, Ms. Kidd?"

I blushed, remembering exactly what Nick and I had been doing. "I forgot where I parked my car," I lied. "Detective, I know you know that Cat and her husband argued at the party the night of his murder. That's all it was—an argument. Their life was about to change significantly and he was looking forward to that. He bought her a mother of pearl baby rattle and a strand of the most gorgeous pearls you've ever seen and he hid them in the house so she wouldn't know. She had no reason to want him dead, but somebody else did."

It was more than a few hours before we were able to leave, not because the police wanted us to stay but because Cat was in no shape to walk. While we sat back, observing the activities around us with nothing other than our own thoughts to serve as distraction, Cat brought up something that had been niggling at the back of my mind.

"Should we tell them about the camera?" she asked. "They're going to find it sooner or later."

I'd been thinking about that camera. Now more than ever I regretted asking Dante to take it away. If it had still been in place, we'd have pictures of who did this.

A numbing feeling started in my torso and then radiated outward through my arms and legs. The tablet was at my house. I'd only gone through a portion of the pictures on it. Now, I wondered at the coincidence of the pearls in the ceiling and the body in her office. They had to be connected.

Cat looked at me, eyes wide. "Why did your face just lose all color?" she asked.

I lowered my voice to just above a whisper. "We need to get to my place and look at those pictures."

I drove to Cat's house. She packed an overnight bag while I cleaned Logan's temporary litterbox and packed him in his carrier. Minutes later, we were en route to my house. Cat was in unchartered territory, and while being in her house might have provided certain comforts, I suspected the reminder of her life with George around every corner would be worse than coming with me.

Plus the shock that goes with finding a body—and realizing that somehow you're now mixed up in a murder investigation—is not always easy to process. That it happened in her store—not once, but twice—made the crimes more personal.

I parked in the driveway. As soon as we were inside the living room I let Logan out of his carrier and he took off. We tossed our coats on top of the sofa and went into the kitchen. "Want anything? Food? Drink?"

"Vodka," Cat said.

"No, seriously."

"I'm being serious. I want vodka. But since I can't have vodka, I'll take a glass of cold water. Just serve it in a martini glass so I can pretend okay?"

"One water in a martini glass coming up." I dug out the glasses and filled them from a pitcher I kept in the fridge. "The computer is upstairs."

"Let's go." Apparently just the illusion of a martini gave her enough courage to face the details behind the dead body in her store.

She headed up the stairs and slowed as she reached the landing. "Which way?" she asked.

"Turn left."

The last time Cat had been in my spare bedroom I'd been using it as a walk-in closet. Racks of off-season clothes had taken up the majority of the space around the small desk that held my PC and printer. In the days between employment opportunities I'd been forced to assess my wardrobe for value and had even sold off a few choice items in order to make my mortgage payment, a process that had pained me greatly. Nobody would treasure those late-Nineties satin cargo pants the way I did.

Since then I'd packed up the garments and stored them in the closet, safe from moths and Logan (he had a thing for cashmere). The desk had expanded thanks to a plank of wood from Lowe's and a couple of wooden sawhorses and was in an L-configuration. I'd upgraded to a twenty-two inch monitor (it was better for shopping on eBay) and an assortment of colorful Sharpies separated into clear vases from the Dollar Store.

The tablet computer that Dante had dropped off sat next to my printer. A thin cord connected the two. I jiggled the mouse to wake up the computer and clicked through the images as they appeared on the screen.

"You don't really think we have a picture of what happened, do you?" Cat asked.

"I don't know. Do we even know what happened? You told Detective Madden that you found Aguilar in your office. How did he get there? Did anybody see him go in? Why was he in there? Has mall security ever gone into your office before? It looks suspicious. Especially after I found the pearls in the ceiling. Did Madden check Aguilar's footprint? Could he have been involved in George's murder? Everything about it points to the fact that he wasn't there because you invited him in."

"That's a lot of questions," Cat said.

"Remember how I told you he was hanging around your store after dark? And that Shana threw something away and he took it out of the trash? That's weird, right? I mean, now that he was found dead in your office."

She lost more coloring. "I'm going to be sick," she said. She ran to the hall bathroom and threw up. The faucet turned on and off. When she returned, she apologized.

"For what? This kind of thing bothers you. That's good. That means you're normal."

"But you can talk about it. You can look at crime scenes and ask questions and suspect people. Why can't I be more like you?"

"Cat, I'm not eight months pregnant." Hearing Cat talk about wanting to be like me cast my whole life in a different light. "I am suspicious by nature," I said. "You know what else? I eat junk food and make decisions other people think are bad. That's who I am. That's not you. I need you to be the person you are: strong, reliable. Practical. Cautious."

"But you get things done."

"I won't let you risk your life because you think you're doing what I would have done."

"But we have an agreement."

"That's not how Life works. You be you and I'll be me. Okay?"

"Okay," she said. I could have sworn a shroud of relief settled in over her shoulders.

"Look carefully at these photos. Tell me if anything looks out of place," I said. The first few images showed Cat entering her office, sitting, working. Business as usual with no big surprises. It was the next series that caught my attention, and apparently hers as well.

We stared at pictures that documented an affair. They grew increasingly intimate, starting with two people entering the office and ending the series with a photo that showed that the woman wore very little under her chinchilla coat. Although knowing her spending habits, I guessed her lingerie cost more than outfits modest people wore in public.

Cat's eyes widened and she put her hand to her mouth in surprise. "Are they going to...?"

"I'm pretty sure they are," I said. "And judging from your expression you're as surprised as I am to see that Jim Insendo was using your office to have an affair with Lela Sexton."

25

I selected the incriminating photos and clicked print. The power button blinked orange and an error message on the screen indicated that the cyan toner was out of ink. I dug a backup cartridge out of a bin and replaced it. The printer recalibrated and then chugged out the photos.

Cat grabbed the stack as they printed and handed them to me. I tapped them on the corner of the desk to line up the edges, and then we moved to the kitchen. Cat bent over and breathed into a paper bag. I called Eddie at Tradava.

"Cat's in trouble. Big trouble. She needs our help."

"Roger that," Eddie said. "I'll be there as soon as the store closes."

Cat pulled a bag of Fritos out of a very large tote bag, dropped the bag onto the sofa, and tore the bag open.

"Are you sure you want to eat like that?" I asked.

"I can't drink. I can't sleep. I can't take Valium or Xanax or Ambien. I spent the morning planning a memorial service for the husband who left me and I can't see my feet." She put a handful of Fritos into her mouth and crunched. "Besides, you would."

"Cat, sit down."

She clutched the bag like Linus with his blanket. I sat next to her. "You've just been through a traumatic situation. There's no doubt of that. I know exactly how you're feeling. I've been there. You barely knew me at the time, but I did exactly what you're doing now."

"What exactly am I doing now?"

"You're trying to hide from the situation. You're hoping it will go away. Don't you remember when I came into your store for the first time and was on a bender of a shopping spree? I wanted to distract myself. Just like you're trying to do now. You don't want to think about it so you're trying to do whatever you can to pretend you didn't discover a dead body in your store. Not just one, but two."

I had to say it, to point out the facts, while I had her attention. When I spoke the last words she reached into the bag of Fritos.

"Cat, here's the deal. Sooner or later you're going to have to do something. It doesn't matter what. You can close the store for the holidays. You can list it for sale. You can sell the house and move. It's your life. You deserve to know what happened, but you don't deserve to be a spectator on the sidelines waiting for someone else to wrap up the details."

She didn't let go of the bag but she didn't pull out more corn chips either. A minute passed. It felt like an hour.

"What do you suggest?"

"We make some coffee—leaded for me and unleaded for you—and go over the photos. Start a timeline of everything that happened. Figure out where we have questions and how we can get answers. Come up with a plan."

Another minute passed. She ate another handful of Fritos. Apparently my little talk hadn't done a bit of good. But then she placed the bag on the table in front of her and looked me straight in the eyes. "Do you have any green vegetables?"

Half an hour later, Eddie arrived. He held two pizza boxes in one hand and a cardboard four pack of Birch Beer in the other. Wedged under his arm was an oversized Post-It board, and his cargo pants fought his belt thanks to the assortment of Sharpies bursting from the pockets. He pushed past us with a few unintelligible grumbles.

"Hello to you too," I said.

"No time for hello." He handed me the pizza boxes (green peppers and basil for Cat, extra cheese for Eddie and me, pepperoni on half to peel off and give to Logan for putting up with us) and took a bottle of Birch Beer out of the cardboard container. He then shoved the remaining three bottles at me. "Fridge." While I refrigerated the soda bottles, he opened up the Post-It pad, tore off a large sheet, and stuck it to my wall. He pulled a Sharpie out of the pocket of his hoodie and wrote, "Suspects," across the top. He repeated the process two more times, writing, "Motive," and "Means." He pulled a bottle opener from his other pocket, popped the top off the birch beer, and swigged from the bottle. When he finished, he pointed at the wall. "Do your thing."

"My thing?" I said. "I don't have a thing."

Cat grabbed the crinkled brown paper bag and started breathing into it again. I pointed to the living room. "We need to talk."

Once we were on the other side of the wall, I turned to him. "'My thing'?" I said, using finger quotes. "In case you haven't noticed, this is no dream. This is really happening!"

"That's from *Rosemary's Baby*, isn't it?" Eddie asked. "You better not let Cat hear you quote that movie."

"I already did," Cat called out from the kitchen.

I put my hand on Eddie's arm and led him to the other side of the Christmas tree. I plugged in the electric train that ran around the perimeter of the tree stand and dropped my voice to just above a whisper. "I'm going to talk fast to get you caught up. Don't interrupt me."

"Go."

"Cat's husband didn't leave her. He left her but then she found a present from him that indicates that he didn't plan to leave her so now we think he pretended to leave to protect her."

"Not abandoned—check."

"But nobody else knows that because right after we discovered the present, I went to Catnip and found the stolen jewelry in the ceiling of Cat's office."

"Stolen jewelry found—check."

"I called the detective to tell him what I knew, but he doesn't know about George not leaving Cat so he not only still thinks she has motive, but now he thinks I hid the jewelry in her ceiling to make it look like somebody else is involved."

"Falsifying evidence—check."

"No! I didn't falsify anything! But he thinks I did because he doesn't know about the baby rattle in the fireplace."

"Baby rattle in the fireplace." He paused. "Dude, you officially stumped my decoder ring."

"That's the present George hid in the fireplace. A baby rattle and a poem. And a pearl necklace for Cat that cost more than my car. But now the security officer who I think maybe helped steal the jewelry in the ceiling is dead and Detective Madden doesn't want to hear about baby rattles and roses being red. Maybe there's a conspiracy at the mall. Or there's a lunatic Santa on the loose. Or maybe one of the other boutique owners are offing the competition?"

"Slow down, Bugsy," Eddie said. He held up his hands like claws and put them on either side of my head. "You need to take all that and sort it out. Because somewhere between the baby rattles and the roses and the pearls and the whatever else you have in there is the answer."

It didn't take long for us to turn the kitchen into a makeshift war room. I was starting to wonder if it made sense to set up an actual crime lab in the house. Not that I was terribly upset about covering up the blue floral wallpaper, but the giant tear-off sheets of notes that now surrounded the room gave it a decidedly graffitied look. Stephen Sprouse meets Martha Stewart.

Cat went to the restroom. We'd finished the pizza, so I refilled Eddie's and my coffee and emptied a fresh bag of pretzels into a bowl.

Eddie bit into a pretzel. "She's doing better than I expected," he said.

"There are a lot of people checking in on her. A lot."

"Like who?"

"Her family, George's family. The neighbors. The company George worked for. Her refrigerator is filled with food that other people brought. How do people know what she likes? Or what she wants to eat?"

"That's what people do." He snapped off another piece of pretzel and chased it with black coffee.

"They do what?"

"They bring casseroles. Stuff that can be frozen so she won't have to worry about cooking. Maybe her close friends will take over her daily errands like laundry and dry cleaning."

"Aren't we her close friends?"

"Yes, but Tradava's got me so busy there's not much I could do other than decorate her house and hire a maid service to clean for her twice a week."

"You hired her a maid service?"

He shrugged. "I wish I could have done more." He took another swig of coffee. "You're helping her with the store, right? That's big."

"I guess so. I'm just trying to be a good friend."

I hadn't heard the toilet flush or the stairs creak, so when Cat spoke behind me, she took me by surprise. "What's this?" she asked. She stood in the doorway. Her palm was face up and the velvet ring box with Nick's engagement ring sat in the center of it.

"It's an engagement ring."

"Nick asked you to marry him?" she asked.

"Yes, but I haven't said yes yet."

"You didn't tell me?"

"I didn't think you'd want to hear about that, not now, not with everything that's happened."

Cat set the ring box down on the bookcase next to her. "I have to go," she said. She pulled on her coat on the way to the front door. I looked at Eddie, expecting him to say something.

He crossed his arms over his chest. "Nick proposed and you didn't tell us?" He stood up. " Cat, hold up. I'll give you a ride."

"Wait!" My chair tipped backward as I stood up and chased after them. "You're crazy busy with Tradava and Cat's got this whole baby-George-pearl thing to worry about! I was trying to be a friend and support you both. Why are you mad?"

The front door was open and Cat was halfway to Eddie's VW Bug. The street lamps were on, backlighting flurries of snow that blew through the wind. Fluffy flakes melted into her red hair on contact. She turned around and faced me. "You're trying so hard to be a good friend but you know what you forgot? How to be a good friend."

"Cat—"

"I lost everything, Sam! My whole life. Don't think that pretending you don't have a life makes any of this easier for me. I don't need you to figure out why George died because that's not going to bring him back. It's not going to change anything."

"But—"

"Do you know what I need? I need life to feel normal. I need for you talk to me about Nick's proposal or to complain about your job or to calculate how many pair of satin cargo pants you need to sell on eBay in order to pay the mortgage. I need you to eat an entire pizza and have room for ice cream. I need to know that some things change and some things never will. Do you get that? I mean, really, Sam. Do you even understand why I'm hurt?"

I looked at Eddie. "She's right, dude. That thing about you saving Nick's dad's life around your birthday? I had to read about that in the paper. If you want people to bring you casseroles when you need them, you're going to have to learn to open up."

"My life is an open book! You two know everything about me."

Cat crossed her arms. "Really? When's the last time you had sex?"

"Excuse me?"

"We're sharing. Friends share. And I'm going to need something really personal to make up for this. So, when's the last time you had sex?"

"Two nights ago in the parking lot of the Ribbon Designer Outlets. It was the night Nick came home from Italy and I convinced him to come with me for overnight surveillance on your store. We got distracted. And oh, by the way, that was our first time and he proposed the next morning and I'm not sure what to make of the timing. Are you happy now?"

Across the street, the front window curtains moved to the side. Mrs. Iova, my occasionally nosy neighbor, stared out at me. I glared at her and then turned around and stormed back into the house.

The kitchen was a mess. Logan was on the dining room table sniffing for leftovers. I moved him to the floor and cleaned up the empty bottles of birch beer that lay scattered next to the pizza boxes. My hands were shaking. The front door opened but I didn't turn around. It wasn't every day that I told the whole neighborhood about my love life, and, frankly, I was a little embarrassed.

"Well, that should be good for a couple of casseroles," Eddie said. He was alone. I looked at the window. "She'll be in in a second. Her phone rang and she wanted some privacy."

"Nice concept."

"Dude, did you hear anything she said to you out there? Because she's right. You're amazing and loyal and you help us all, but the reason we're friends is because you're kind of a mess."

"Thanks a lot."

"No, seriously. Listen to me. I'm a mess too. I'm a single guy who spends three quarters of my life at my job. I don't even have a pet. The most exciting thing to happen to me this month was to win an auction of an original red Devo Energy Dome on eBay."

"You mean one of those flowerpot hats?"

"Energy Dome, dude. I could have gotten a flower pot for a lot less."

"You didn't tell me about that."

"Because that being the most exciting thing in my life is pathetic. But you and Nick? That's been over a decade in the making."

The front door opened a second time and Cat walked in. This time she wasn't alone. Detective Madden was behind her.

"Ms. Kidd," he said. He stepped forward and held his hand out to Eddie. "Detective Madden."

"Eddie Adams," Eddie replied.

"He called," Cat said to me. "I gave him your address and told him to come here."

The four of us stood around my living room. Detective Madden was the last person I'd expect to show up at my house tonight, but I was having a hard time regrouping on details of the investigation thanks to Cat and Eddie.

"Detective, would you like a cup of coffee?" Cat asked.

"Do you have decaf?"

"Yes. Follow me." Cat headed toward the kitchen. When she passed me, she reached out her hand and put it on my hand and squeezed. I looked at her face. She smiled a genuine smile that let me know we were going to be okay. I squeezed back. She let go and Madden followed her into the kitchen. About two seconds later, Madden asked, "What's all this?"

Oh, crap! The wall of observation!

I ran into the kitchen. Cat handed Madden a mug of coffee. Madden thanked her and looked at the giant Post-It sheets that hung from the wall. His eyes scanned from the left page to the right, pausing on the photo of Lela Sexton in her lingerie. Between the scene out front and the wall of observation in my kitchen, my secrets were pretty much out in the open.

"Don't mind the mess," I said quickly. I grabbed the packages of giant Post-Its and covered the existing wall of observation with blank sheets. "We're helping Cat work out her staffing issues."

He held his mug, but didn't drink from it. "Sorry to drop in unexpected, but I thought you'd want to know that we ran tests on your gun and it came back clean. Hasn't been fired in some time."

"I already told you that," Cat said.

"And I appreciate your honesty, Ms. Lestes, but I hope you understand we have to follow procedure. You can pick it up at the station at your convenience."

"I don't want it. I never wanted it," Cat said. "Is that all?"

"No, there's something else. A pretty significant break in our investigation, actually, although I'm not really sure what it means yet. Ms. Lestes, your store is going to have to be closed indefinitely."

"I haven't been back, not since the second murder," she said. "I already told my staff so there's no reason anybody would try to open the store until I contact them."

"That's just the thing. A member of your staff threw us this new curve ball."

"I'm sorry, detective. I don't follow."

"Your assistant manager, Shana Brice, came to see us this afternoon. She said it's time she told us the truth. And then she gave us a full confession."

26

"Shana killed my husband?" Cat asked. She sank down into a dining room chair. Eddie stood behind her and put his hands on her shoulders.

"No, ma'am, she confessed to the burglaries. Seems she and Mr. Aguilar have been stealing from the mall on a pretty regular basis. Small, petty thefts originally intended to help complete their holiday shopping that turned into a way to profit on the side. Mr. Aguilar got her into the mall after hours. Ms. Brice committed the actual thefts. She put the stolen merchandise in a bag and threw it out in a public trash can. Mr. Aguilar retrieved it from the designated spot and they reconvened after hours to divvy up the goods."

"But Cat started to carry more expensive jewelry," I said. "A fact Shana would know because she worked there. She'd know where it was kept and how much it was worth. Even if it was locked up at night, she'd be able to get at it."

"She said she learned the true value of the new merchandise at the party that night."

"Shana wasn't at the party," Cat said.

"She was the woman in the restroom," I said slowly. Now I realized why Shana had seemed familiar to me when I first met her at Catnip. "I didn't put two and two together. She was all dressed up, not in goth attire. Her hair wasn't blue, and she took out her piercings."

"I think I still would have recognized her," Cat said.

"When I saw her talking to George, I feared the worst—that maybe he was having an affair—so I kept you distracted so you wouldn't see her."

"The two of them had gotten away with smaller thefts for weeks," Madden said, "and had a false sense of confidence in the simplicity of their plan. Ms. Brice could have stolen the jewelry during her shift, but that night she waited until after the mall closed. Aguilar told her security would be busy with the party. He volunteered to cover the rest of the mall so she wouldn't have to worry about being caught. It was risky, but the temptation of stealing merchandise of that value was too great. For someone who carried a healthy amount of credit card debt, the take was potentially life-changing."

"And the murder? How did she do that?" I asked.

"She claims she didn't have anything to do with the murder. We drilled her about that pretty well and her story never changed. She was in the store. She smashed a case of jewelry with the tire iron. That's when she saw the body. You screamed and it snapped her out of shock. She was afraid you were the killer. She grabbed the jewelry and ran, knocking Ms. Lestes out of the way in the process. We checked her footprint against the print we found in the carpet and it's a match."

"Why didn't she say anything before now?"

"For the past several days, she kept quiet because her confession didn't cast her in innocent light. But when Mr.

Aguilar was found dead in Ms. Lestes's office, she looked at things differently."

"She thought Cat killed George?"

"That is her opinion. She came to us to point the finger at Ms. Lestes."

I didn't like it. Cat was at the store the night George was murdered, but so was Shana. Cat had access to her own office, but so did Shana. The only person who could have fingered Shana as having been there was Aguilar—who was now dead.

"What do you think?" I asked Madden.

"I have to admit, her statement confuses things." He set his mug down on the table. He zipped his coat and pulled on a hat. "I'll be on my way now. Heard there's a storm coming. Oh, Ms. Kidd, we caught the vandals responsible for your flat tire. I never saw your report but I thought you'd want to know. You three take care." He shook each of our hands and then left.

I wasn't buying Madden's whole "just happened to discover" this and "thought you'd want to know" that. It was all too convenient.

We returned to my dining room table. I took down the blank Post-It sheets and we stared at the wall of observation. Despite several rounds of "Did-Shana-do-it?" Eddie remained unconvinced.

"She described in detail what was stolen," I continued. "She even said I almost caught her. She dropped a necklace in the public bathroom the night of the party. I picked it up and handed it to her. She told Madden that she was scared I figured it out so she panicked and threw it away right in front of me."

Reasoning through the rest of the details after reaching this conclusion raised a whole other set of questions.

"Cat, how much of your jewelry assortment was stolen?"

"A lot."

"No, you misunderstand me. What's the value? Ballpark."

Her eyes rolled up toward the ceiling and her head bounced back and forth while she did some mental math. "About thirty-four thousand dollars retail, unless you want cost."

"I thought you owned an outlet. How come you have such expensive stuff?"

"Technically it's an outlet, but I prefer the term 'off-price retailer.'"

"What's the difference?" Eddie asked.

"An outlet sells last season's merchandise, stuff that's been severely discounted because it's not current. I get that merchandise from jobbers—people who buy end of season merchandise from department stores. I usually buy entire lots of product sight unseen. The jobbers sell it by a piece count. Like, two hundred pair of jeans, or thirty designer handbags, or something like that. There's always a gamble with jobbers, because if the price is right and the description sounds good I'll take it, but it's mine to either sell or throw away."

Eddie got up and refilled his coffee.

"What about the rest of your inventory?" I asked.

"Mostly off-price. I go to market and visit with designers and vendors. Sometimes they end up with overruns of merchandise that didn't sell, that they produced to meet minimums. Sometimes stores negotiate inventory returns to them for various reasons. If I have good relationships with the vendors that I want to carry, they know they can call me and I might buy that inventory discounted. That way they're getting more than if they had to sell it to a jobber or at a sample sale."

"What about the jewelry? Didn't you tell me you came up with a luxury goods strategy recently and that's why you bought the pearls from Kenner & Winn?"

"It was something like that. I noticed about a year ago that there weren't any good jewelry stores in the designer outlets, so I started bumping up my average price to test the waters. Nothing too classic, but pieces that I found in the market. A few designers were willing to work on consignment. The merchandise sold so I gradually built up the category. I knew I could go to the five hundred dollar range. George's inventory was a risk. Those pieces were a couple thousand dollars cost, even with a discount. I told you my terms were Net 30, so I had thirty days to pay the invoice. The risk was whether I'd sell the jewelry before the bill was due. I thought I could because of the time of the year."

Eddie and I exchanged glances. I knew what he was thinking. "So you don't normally carry this much jewelry?" he asked.

"Oh, God no. I usually have a couple of necklaces and earrings and an assortment of bangles. Very minimalist. I arranged through the outlet center to have extra jewelry cases put into the store so I could carry more merchandise this month."

"Did the rest of your assortment change much? Because of the holidays?"

"Not really. Like I said, it's an outlet, but also an off-price store. I change the way I merchandise some things, but other than the jewelry it's still the same."

"Who else knew about your business strategy?"

"I asked Shana to come with me to select the merchandise. I thought it would be a nice opportunity for her since she doesn't get out of the store much." She looked dazed. "I tried to help her with her professional growth and she thanked me by stealing from my store and then implicating me in the murder of my husband. What kind of a world do we live in?"

Eddie leaned forward. "What do you think about this?" he asked me. "Do you believe her confession?"

"I don't believe anything any of these people say," I said, gesturing toward our wall of observation. "Shana confessed because it was the safest thing for her to do. But I saw her talk to George at the party. And before you say it, it wasn't like she was talking to her boss's wife. They *knew each other* knew each other."

Cat spoke in a low voice. "I told George I was going to Catnip after the party. I think he went there to tell me what was really going on. You took a long time to get to the store because you had to get your underwear out of the bushes, remember?"

I pointed a finger at Eddie. "Don't ask."

He held both hands up in mock surrender. "Dude."

"Shana was there to steal from you. She knew the lights would be out and she thought you were at the party. Maybe George knew what she had planned. Maybe he went to stop her. He could have overpowered her. He could have pulled off the mask, and maybe she killed him because he could identify her." And then she realized she could easily frame Cat for everything. Everything was falling into place.

We hashed things out into the wee hours of the morning. I told Cat and Eddie to go to sleep, but my mind was alert. I didn't want to tell either of them, but Shana's confession still troubled me. Why had someone knotted the pearls around George's throat after shooting him? And why hide the merchandise in the ceiling if she intended to confess? There were other details just slightly out of reach in my mind, that I knew I was missing. The information felt like chapters pulled from several different novels.

I let Cat and Eddie sleep while I tossed and turned, trying to make the pieces fit. They needed it. Eddie was exhausted thanks to the grueling hours he kept at Tradava. Cat was living through a nightmare. It was like we'd traded lives: me with the solid job, the promising relationship, and the financial security. Her unexpectedly on her own weeks before having a baby, her store on the brink of financial ruin. For as long as I'd known her, I'd thought she had it all. If everything could change in an instant, then wasn't the illusion of security a farce?

27

TUESDAY EARLY MORNING

There would be no sleeping in on my vacation. I woke first and left Cat and Eddie a note. Eddie's VW Bug was in the driveway so I took his keys and drove to the closest bagel store. I bought breakfast sandwiches for each of us: eggs Florentine for Cat (spinach), egg white, gluten-free (no flavor) for Eddie, and double bacon, egg, and cheese (yum!) for me. The wind was picking up, and I struggled to keep the VW in my lane.

It was too early for the color that the sky had turned. A snowstorm was definitely coming. Nostalgia tugged at my heart. It would be nice to have the world blanketed in pure white. Mother Nature's way of hiding all of the imperfections on the landscape of life.

I turned right at the restaurant on the corner and drove down the street, lost in thoughts of snowmen and icicles. It was the navy blue sedan, parked where Eddie's VW had been, that pulled me back to reality. Who was visiting now?

I approached the front door with caution. I shouldn't have left Cat alone, even for only a few minutes. The doorknob turned easily under my hand, which meant someone had left it unlocked. I entered and called out a tentative hello.

"In here," Cat replied from the kitchen.

Jim sat across the table from Cat.

He pushed his chair back and stood up. "Samantha," he said. "Nice to see you again."

"Sure. I mean, you too." Considering the photos I'd seen of him and Lela, I had a hard time making eye contact. "Where's Eddie?"

"In the shower," Cat said.

"If I'd have known you were coming, I would have gotten you a bagel."

"Don't apologize. I don't eat bread," He said, holding both hands up. "With what happened at the store yesterday, I thought maybe you forgot to give Cat the envelope I gave you. I called her and she invited me here. I hope you don't mind."

"Of course not," I lied. Everybody knew I loved having sexed up murder suspects sitting around my dining room table. Especially ones who don't eat carbs.

He turned to Cat. "Think about what I said. It might be exactly what you need." He buttoned up his coat and picked up a brown wool hat from the table. "I'll let myself out," he said. "Bye, Samantha."

I waited until the front door closed behind him to drop into the chair across from her. "He gave me something to give you. I forgot. I'm sorry." I craned my neck to read the papers in front of her from my upside down angle. "What is that?"

"It's an offer to buy back the store."

"From Jim?"

She nodded. "He said he's been thinking maybe he'd made a mistake when he sold me the store. He's bored. He never expected that. I guess that's the thing about retail. It's a high-stress, high paced job and certain types of people are drawn to it, but the burn-out rate is high too. People are always happy when they get out, but in time they discover this huge gaping hole in their lives because suddenly everyone isn't coming after them to solve their problems."

"Is that how he described it?"

"No, that's my own interpretation," she said.

I powered up the tablet and swiped through the pictures of him and Lela quickly and then slowed by the ones after both had left. About twenty images later, I spotted something we'd missed.

"Look at this. These pictures are from after Jim and Lela left."

I spun the tablet Cat's direction. We'd already seen that Jim and Lela had been having an affair, conducted, at times, in Cat's office. We had *not* seen Lela return to the office by herself. But the camera had caught her rifling through Cat's desk.

"Didn't you say Lela used to work at the store?" I asked.

"Yes, when Jim owned it."

"How often does she go into your office?"

"I never knew she did until now."

"What do you think she's doing?"

"I have no idea."

"Did she know about your jewelry strategy?"

"No, but I told Jim," she said. "At the party." She dropped her eyes. "I just wanted someone to talk to."

"Did you tell him before or after he gave you an offer to buy back the store?"

She didn't answer.

"Today wasn't the first time he's brought up buying you out, is it?"

"No," she confessed.

"Did Jim say anything about Lela?" I stood up and approached the wall of observation. We'd labeled Lela a suspect and had pinned an incriminating photo of the two of them about to bring up the natural shine on Cat's desk. The photo was missing, as was the sheet with Lela's name.

"I thought it best not to let him see that we knew about that. When he arrived, I asked him to wait out front for a second. I said I was getting off the phone, but I came in here and took the notes down."

"Good thinking."

Cat silently stared at the table. "I talked to my parents last night. Their flight was canceled because of the weather. As soon as this is over I'm going to go stay with them."

She looked at me. The events of the past few days had taken their toll on her and it was starting to show. There were dark circles under her eyes, her usually peaches and crème complexion had taken on a dull gray shade, and her normally erect posture had converted to slumped shoulders. She seemed defeated. How could she not? Every single thing she knew about her life had changed—except for the one thing that was going to change in the next month. Cat was the one person who seemed to have it all, but in the blink of an eye, she was on the verge of having nothing.

28

The snowstorm started sometime during breakfast. At first, it was a couple of flurries. We gathered around the windows and watched, temporarily distracted by the miracle of nature. Thin flakes turned into fatter ones that coated the street. After forty-five minutes, it was undeniable. Our stretch of unseasonably warm weather in December had broken and this storm wasn't going to subside for a while.

"I'm due at Tradava," Eddie said. "At this rate they're going to close, but I'm a member of senior management and probably the closest person to the store. Somebody has to be there to decide whether to open or close and if I leave it up to one of the merchandise managers, they'll argue that we need the sales." He pulled on his thick ski jacket. "Cat, do you want a ride?"

"I'm not on the way."

"No, but if we leave now, I can get to your house and back to the store pretty quickly. Much longer and the roads are going to be too slick."

They collected their things and left. Logan jumped onto the arm of my chair and climbed to the top of it. He ran his head across my nose and then gingerly stepped onto the white windowsill and lowered himself. Logan loved snowstorms, as long as he wasn't required to go outside in them.

I cleaned up as best as I could and then sat at the kitchen table and stared at the wall of observation. Could Shana be telling the truth? I didn't know. But if Shana truly believed that Cat was responsible for the murders, then both of their lives were in danger.

Despite the coffee, the questions, the snowstorm, and the general sense of unease, I fell asleep on the sofa. I woke to the sound of knocking on the front door. The room was dark. I got up and turned on the lamp on my end table. The switch clicked, but nothing happened. I moved to the wall and tried the dimmer. Nothing.

The knock continued. I moved to the window, cupped my hands around my eyes, and looked outside. Nick's truck was in my driveway. The rest of the neighborhood had been blanketed in white, creating an innocent setting. It was odd how peaceful it appeared in direct contrast to the crime wave at the outlets.

I opened the door and let Nick in. "Why's it so dark in here?" He was bundled up in a cranberry hat, plaid scarf, and navy blue pea coat.

"The power must have gone out." I flicked the light switch a few times to demonstrate. "How'd you get here?" I asked. "I mean, I know you drove, but it looks pretty bad out there."

"I have snow tires on my car. You okay? I tried calling a few times but the call went straight to voicemail."

"The battery was low. I plugged it in, but if the power went out then it couldn't charge." I headed to the kitchen. "Do you want some coffee? It's probably cold but it's relatively fresh."

Nick hung his coat on the back of a kitchen chair and set his hat, gloves, and scarf on the table. His eyes swept over the walls, taking in Dante's surveillance photos, the scribbled identifications, and our lists of clues, notes, and questionable activity. I was about to repeat my question when he replied.

"You need a shower. I'll get the coffee."

Alrighty-then.

The steaming water caressed my aching shoulders and back and I found myself becoming more aware of how little quality sleep I'd gotten of late. My mind became a blank canvas, absorbing the relaxing sensation of the shower beating down on me. Eventually the water turned cooler, a sign that the water heater was getting low. I got out, dried off and wrapped my hair up in the towel turban-style, and pulled on a plush robe.

The long shower had a side effect on me. Not only had it relaxed my muscles and settled my brain, it drained my last drops of energy. I was dizzy from the change in temperature and needed to sit down. I pulled the covers back from the bed and crawled between the sheets, resting my head against the pillow. I just needed a few minutes. I closed my eyes.

It was dark. I didn't want to be awake. I shut my eyes and nestled further between the cozy down covers. A pair of arms encircled me, and I let out a quiet, sleepy moan as I readjusted my position. About a half second later my eyes popped open and I went rigid. Nick was next to me.

He pulled me close, holding me as though he wasn't going to let go. We lay like that for a while, no questions, no answers, no danger.

I told him about the last twenty-four hours: Shana's confession, Detective Madden's visit, George's hidden presents left behind in the fireplace, Jim and Lela's affair in Cat's office. Every time I hesitated before sharing more details he gently encouraged me to continue. It felt good to talk to him, to let it all out.

When I finished (more like when I finally paused for air), I wondered what was going through his mind. The longer we lay in silence, the more I worried that I'd said too much. Logan, not one recognize a moment when he sees it, chose that moment to howl for his dinner.

"I think you better get up and feed your cat."

"Can't we stay like this for a couple more minutes?" I mumbled, attempting to ignore the persistent cries from the floor.

"I'm not sure that's such a good idea."

"Logan's on a diet. He's not going to starve."

"I was referring to the fact that you're very naked underneath that robe. Unless you want to conduct some more overnight surveillance..."

29

TUESDAY EVENING

"Now, who are these people?" Nick asked. We were in the kitchen. After our bedroom tryst, I dressed in a leopard printed cashmere lounging tunic and pants. We each held a flashlight aimed at the wall of observation. I'd also dug up a laser pointer that doubled as Logan's favorite toy and used it to pinpoint different facts.

"That's Jim Insendo, the man Cat bought the boutique from, and that's Lela Sexton, one of Cat's employees," I said.

"They seem to like each other."

I nodded. Standing in the kitchen bringing Nick up to speed on the investigation was one thing, but staring at the intimate photos of Jim and Lela, especially after just climbing out of bed with Nick, was a little uncomfortable (in a good way).

"So what's their connection to Cat's husband?"

"It's complicated. Jim used to own Cat's store. He offered to buy the boutique back from Cat just recently. See that picture of Lela leaving Cat's office? We think she might have planted something on Cat's desk, or taken documents from her office, so she would be more prone to sell."

"Is she? Considering selling the store?"

I nodded. "I can't tell if it's because she really wants to or if everything is getting to her. The week before Christmas is stressful for anybody who works retail. She's got so much extra piled on top of that stress that who knows why she's doing what she's doing."

Nick scanned the wall. "Kenner & Winn...the jewelry wholesalers? Why did you write their names up there?"

"We don't have pictures of them."

"What do they have to do with this?"

"George worked for them. How do you know them?"

"Industry connections. I meet a lot of these people on the accessories circuit. So the pearls that were stolen from Cat's store the night of his murder came from their inventory?" I nodded. "Which means they knew the value of the merchandise at the store."

"Yes."

"Do you trust them?"

"Seems doubtful they'd be involved. Why rob the store of merchandise they could get on their own? Why commit murder at all? If it's about the pearls, they can mine more."

"You think pearls come from a mine like diamonds?" He smiled.

"You know what I meant. Winn's been out of the country this whole time. And Tom Kenner offered to pay for all of George's funeral services and three months' salary to help Cat."

"Okay, let's get back to Cat. Somebody went out of their way to pull her into this thing. Any idea why?"

"That's what I originally thought, but now I'm not sure. The more I think about George, the more I wonder why was he killed? It doesn't make sense that it was a case of mistaken identity, because why else would he have been at Catnip that night? Somebody arranged for him to show up, and whoever that was must have planned to kill him. If it's about George, that's one thing. But the security officer was murdered too. What's the connection between them? Anything? Or was it totally random?"

Nick leaned back. "Are you seriously entertaining that as a possibility? Because if that's the case we can forget the whole thing and go out for pizza."

"Don't try to distract me with pizza. I've considered it as a possibility, but not seriously, and here's why. The pearls showed back up in Cat's office. They were stashed in the ceiling. And Aguilar was strangled with a strand of pearls that I had on hold, and if I had them on hold then they couldn't have been stolen in the smash and grab."

He stared at me. "You were going to buy the necklace that the security officer was strangled with?" Our eyes connected. "Do you think that's some kind of sign?"

"No, I think it's bad clothing karma that came back to haunt me. Maybe the fact that I once wore knickers." I chewed my lip. "But I think it means something."

Soon enough the coffee pot was empty and because of the storm there would be no calls for takeout. Nick walked to the pantry and scanned the shelves. I was embarrassed by the fact that I had no food and said as much. My comments were unanswered.

"Keep talking," he said.

"About what? My lack of food?"

"No, about the investigation. Things you've figured out." He pulled a couple of cans from the shelves and set them on the counter. Confused, I tried to regain my earlier train of thought but failed.

"What are you doing?"

"Making us something to eat."

"I don't have any food here."

"You've got plenty of food. You shop like you're preparing for a zombie apocalypse." He held up a couple of cans of spinach. "You expecting Popeye for a visit?"

This whole meal thing had captured my interest, much to Nick's amusement. He turned toward me with his hands propped on the counter.

"I left some parmesan cheese in the fridge. We need to eat it or it'll go bad. I'm going to make pasta and spinach pesto. Will that be to your liking?"

"Sure, yep, sounds good. You can do that without electricity?"

"You have a gas stove and a battery-operated coffee grinder, right?"

I was starting to feel like I had MacGyver in my kitchen. "Right."

While Nick moved about the kitchen, I poured a small bowl of milk for Logan. Nick filled a pot with water and set it on a gas burner. He drained a can of spinach and dumped it into my coffee grinder with olive oil, juice from half a lemon, minced garlic, and some grated cheese. I let him cook in silence while I fished out some candles from the junk drawer. Sooner than expected he brought two steaming plates full of pasta tossed in a green sauce over to the table and sat down across from me. Not a moment too soon, either, since my stomach let out a massive rumble. We spent the next few minutes eating.

"Is there anything else you haven't told me?" he asked.

Dante's face popped into my head. While it might not have been what Nick was asking, it was something I had to confess. "The photos on the wall were taken by Cat's brother. Dante. He's been helping us—her. Us." I paused. "He kissed me two nights ago."

Nick slowly nodded. He set his fork down and put his elbows on the table, and then rested his forehead against his clasped hands. A few seconds later he looked up at me. I laid my arm out on the table with my hand open toward him. He dropped his arm and took my fingers in his. I never looked away from his eyes.

"Nick, I think maybe we're not ready for the next step."

"Are you saying no?"

"I'm saying I need more time. Does this change anything?"

"Not for me."

We finished dinner and turned our attention back to the wall of observation. I stood next to the giant Post-Its and tapped the notes and photos one at a time, giving Nick the necessary bullet points.

"Every suspicious thing we've come to see, hear, suspect, or learn is written up." A thumbtack fell out of the wall at that moment, and a still shot of Cat's office fluttered gently onto the table.

"Okay, so let's see if I get this. This is Jim, the former owner, and he's with Lela, one of Cat's employees. And they seem to be having some sort of affair. Is he married?"

"I don't know."

"Okay, so that may or may not mean anything. Let's move on. Who's the punk girl?"

"Shana Brice. Cat's assistant. She confessed two nights ago."

"If she confessed, why are we talking about this?"

"Because she confessed to stealing the pearls, not the murder. She said she and Aguilar had been stealing all along but that George's body was in the jewelry case when she got there."

"Do you believe her?"

BUY·A·BOOK

and help keep your
library's shelves filled.

BUY A BOOK

In memory of someone,
to honor a birth, confirmation,
wedding, bar/bat mitzvah,
graduation, or an anniversary.
Celebrate a special occasion —
Mother's Day, Father's Day,
birthday, etc.

It's easy to put more books
on the shelves—become a

"Not sure. She said she and Aguilar conspired to steal the pearls. When Aguilar was found dead, Shana got scared and confessed." I shook my head. "Why say anything at that point? If the goal all along was to steal the pearls, then she was in the clear. Why bring them back to the scene of the crime? Why go to such lengths to hide them once they're there? And who killed Aguilar?"

"It's almost like there were two different crimes committed that night," Nick said. I looked at him. We stood facing each other for upwards of a minute. "What?" he finally asked.

"That would explain a lot. Assuming Shana was the thief, she looked...confused. She held a tire iron that I'm pretty sure she used to smash the case. So why would she strangle George?" I was excited by this new theory. My voice picked up and I thought through other details out loud. "She would have had to smash the case so it didn't look like an inside job. It's like *My Cousin Vinny!*"

"There were no metallic mint green convertibles. There were no cans of tuna. How is it like *My Cousin Vinny?*"

"There were two sets of people in the store. The first person killed George. I don't know who, when, or why, but he strangled George and then left his body behind the jewelry case. The second person, Shana, was there to steal the pearls. She broke in and went to the case. She probably knew exactly which case to smash, so she did, but after the crash, she noticed the body. And when I yelled, she turned around and looked at me. She knew I saw her. Even though she was wearing a black mask, she might have thought I could identify her—and now it wouldn't be in conjunction with a smash and grab, it would be with a murder."

"So she took off. And after the fact, with an investigation in full swing, she tried to get the merchandise back to the store to eliminate the evidence."

"She didn't just try, she succeeded."

Nick crossed his arms. "So it's possible that Shana's telling the truth that she committed the thefts but not the murder. Do you believe her?"

"Yes, well, no."

"That's clear."

"Shana—and all of Cat's staff—has access because they have keys. Jim has keys because he's the former store owner and Cat never changed the locks. Aguilar had access to the mall master keys. What if..." I chewed my lip, wondering how crazy Nick was going to think I was when I said this next bit. "What if Shana wasn't trying to hide the pearls in the ceiling? What if she was trying to return the pearls to the store and just didn't have a chance to finish what she started? Like she gained entrance to the store through the ceiling?"

"Kidd, people don't go crawling through ceilings."

"River Phoenix did in *Sneakers*."

He uncrossed his arms and put his hands on either side of my face, bent down, and kissed me.

"What was that for?" I asked.

"Sometimes with you, there are no words."

I refilled our wine and we sat down next to each other facing the wall of observation. "Everything Shana said makes sense. It is entirely possible that she was only there to steal the pearls."

"And her partner, Aguilar? Could he have done it?"

"He came into the store after the crash. So in the case of George's death, I can't get him there."

"They could have killed him earlier."

"True, but then why kill Aguilar? And then why confess at all? Which brings me to Jim. He had a way to get in and he seems awfully persistent about getting the store back. If it's all about running a store, he could just open a different boutique and become one of Cat's competitors."

"You think there's something about that particular store that he's after."

"Yep. I think we're missing something about Catnip."

30

"You mean, why is Cat's store so valuable?" Nick asked.

"Yes. And is it the contents of the store or the *location* of the store?"

"So assume we're missing something about the location. It stands to reason that it's in one of these pictures. Tell me again how"—Nick paused for a fraction of a second—"Cat's brother got these pictures?"

"Dante programmed computer tablets to take pictures every five minutes."

"How many tablets?"

"Two."

"That's five hundred seventy six pictures a day."

"How did you do that?" I demanded.

"What?"

"That math. Right there. Without a calculator."

"Twenty four hours times sixty minutes an hour divided by five minute intervals times two."

"Maybe I'm better at discounts." I unlocked the tablet and handed it to Nick. "You can swipe through the images we didn't print."

"Where's the other one?"

"Upstairs in the walk-in closet on the desk."

He handed the tablet back to me. "I'll be right back."

I studied the pictures again while he was gone. He was right; there had to be something we were missing about Catnip and it had to be right in front of us. I stepped on a thumbtack, cursed, and stooped to pick it up. While I waited for Nick's return I squeezed between the unoccupied chairs on the far side of the table. It was a tighter squeeze than when I tried to get between Cat's desk and file cabinet in her office. I was going to have go back on the Logan half-portion diet for a while.

I stuck the thumbtack into the wall and noticed something we'd all missed. Between the early set of photos and the later ones, the file cabinet in Cat's office had moved. Dante, Cat, Eddie, and I would never have noticed it. Our investigation had become so distracted by the players in the photos that it had never occurred to us to stop and look at the backdrop: Cat's store and office. But once I did, it became obvious that the answer had been there all along.

Other than the location of George's body, Cat's office was the epicenter of the suspicious activity: The necklaces turning up. The location of the affair. Lela stealing something from Cat's desk. Aguilar's body.

When Nick returned to the kitchen, I told him what I discovered. "Cat's office furniture was moved. Look." I pointed to the file cabinet in one photo and then in another. "We have to go to the mall and find out why. We've got to see what's really behind that file cabinet."

"How are you going to get into the store? Do you have keys?"

"Yes, but I need to talk to Cat first." I grabbed my phone before remembering it was dead.

Nick held his out to me. "Do you know the number?"

I pulled out my old phone and looked up the number in my contacts. I accessed the call log on Nick's phone. The most recent call made was to "The Future Mrs. Taylor." I snuck a peek at him to see if he was watching me. He was. He smiled like we shared a secret the rest of the world knew nothing about. I smiled back and felt warm and tingly all the way to my toes.

Focus, Samantha.

I called Cat. "Sam? Is everything okay?" she asked.

"Yes and no and yes. I'm here with Nick and we figured something out. Did Detective Madden release the store to you yet?"

"Yes, but with the storm coming, the mall's closed. Why?"

I looked at Nick. "Do you mind if we check on it? I still have your keys from the night Dante and I reset the store." Nick crossed his arms and frowned slightly. "Okay, thanks." I hung up. "We cleaned up after the police released the crime scene. You were in Italy with Amanda. I don't want to hear a word."

"What? I didn't say anything. Let's go."

I changed into jeans and a turtleneck sweater, pulled on Moon Boots and a white puffer jacket, and followed Nick to his truck.

It took longer than usual to get to the outlet center. I plugged my Nick Phone into his cigarette lighter. Even though the streets had been plowed and showered with salt, Nick drove with caution. Several traffic lights had defaulted to flashing red. The mall was dark, as were the surrounding streetlights and holiday decorations.

The parking lot was mostly empty. A couple of cars remained behind, covered by snow. I pulled on pink mittens and a matching hat and held my coat closed by my neckline. Falling flakes had multiplied, and the wind blew them at an angle past my face. I jumped out of the truck.

I tried to walk faster but the snow hindered my progress. Nick caught up with me and grabbed my elbow. I pulled away but he had a tight grip. I slipped and fell. Nick landed on top of me.

"Stay down," he said.

Gunshots punctured the air. I heard a pop and a sizzle. It was cold. I wriggled around to get out from under him but quickly realized he had me pinned. A car drove past us and lost control in a wide spin around the side of the mall. We jumped up and ran as fast as possible to the entrance. I fumbled and dropped the keys twice before unlocking the door.

"Give me your phone," Nick said.

I held it out. Nick flipped to the contacts, paused at one of the names, looked at me, and then pressed the screen. "Unlock the door," he said to me. "I'll be right back." He turned around. I couldn't hear his voice. A few seconds later he hung up and handed the phone to me.

"Cat's office is on the left side of the store." I pointed. "Come with me."

The door to Cat's office was open. Nick turned on the flashlight and aimed it up. "You said the pearls fell out of the ceiling, right?"

"Right."

"Then let's see what else is up there." He climbed on the desk and pushed two of the cork tiles out of place. He did a pull-up from the metal frame. He stayed there for a few seconds and then dropped back down to the desk.

"Give me a boost," he said.

"Let me go. I'm lighter."

"Don't take this the wrong way, but can you do a pull-up?"

"Fine." I stood on the desk and laced my fingers together. Nick put his foot on my hands and did another pull-up and, with the resistance I provided him, was able to climb up. He disappeared into the ceiling.

"Hey, River, see anything suspicious?" I asked.

His voice came back muffled. "I knew you were going to say that."

While I waited, I stared at the carpet. There was a faint impression, slightly off center from the base of the filing cabinet. I looked up at the ceiling. "I found something down here," I called up.

I set my phone on Cat's desk and tipped the tall, metal file cabinet to the right, revealing a faded square of drywall behind it. I applied pressure on the square and it popped out and fell backward. I grabbed my phone and stepped through. On the floor in front of me was a strand of black pearls. They were far more lustrous than the ones I'd put on hold. I aimed the light at them and they took on a greenish-blue cast. I scooped them up and shoved them into the pocket of my coat.

I was inside the camping store where I'd bought my rain boots for my night with Dante and the blankets for my night with Nick. Slowly, I crept forward, stumbling thanks to the clunkiness of my Moon Boots. The retractable metal gate that separated the store from the mall was open. A beam of light cut its way through the dark interior. I hid next to a display of men's plaid flannel shirts and strained to see who was with me.

Joyce Kenner.

She aimed her flashlight at the ground. I was struck by the odd manner that she held it, until I realized it was taped to something.

A gun.

It was tiny. It looked like a toy. I didn't know squat about guns, but I couldn't see that one inflicting enough damage to take a life.

But in a match of gun vs. pearl necklace, gun would win. The only way I was going to get out of this was to use the element of surprise. I crawled backward past a camping tent and called Nick. A few seconds later, his ringtone sounded from somewhere above me. Joyce pointed her gun/flashlight at the ceiling and fired. The bullet zinged off a length of exposed pipe. I couldn't let her shoot again—not at Nick, who had no idea we were down here.

"Get help," I whispered into the phone and then stood up. "Looking for something?" I asked. Joyce turned toward me and the gun/flashlight followed. "You've gone to a lot of trouble for a strand of pearls that you dropped behind a file cabinet."

She looked surprised to find me there. I didn't know if Nick had heard me. Why hadn't we called the police when we arrived? When the shots were fired in the parking lot? Even if Nick could call them now, would the weather keep them away?

I pulled the black pearls out of my pocket. "These aren't like the other pearls that George placed in Cat's inventory, are they? They don't look like regular pearls." I rested them in my open palm. "They don't feel like regular pearls."

Joyce lunged forward and grabbed for the necklace. I swung my hand back out of reach. "Cat said the order she bought from George was worth about thirty thousand dollars retail. The whole order." I held up the necklace. "I'm guessing this strand is worth a bit more than that, isn't it?"

"Give them to me." She lunged toward me again and I yanked them back. "Two people have died over that necklace. What makes you think you won't be number three?"

"Out of curiosity, what *are* they worth?" I was stalling for time to give Nick a chance to get away. Joyce had acknowledged the murders. She had no intention of letting me walk away.

"It took five years to produce that necklace," said a weak voice from the floor behind her. I craned my neck and saw Tom Kenner leaning against a wooden picnic table. The light from my phone illuminated a dark shiny substance on the thigh of his trousers. "They're natural pearls produced from wild oysters. Gem quality. That strand is worth close to a million dollars."

31

TUESDAY, REALLY LATE

"You— shut up!" Joyce yelled at her husband. "You did this when you slept with that woman. You were supposed to fix this. Now I have to clean up your mess." Joyce looked at me. "Give me the necklace."

"You'll get the pearls when I get answers," I said. "Why did you kill George? What did he do to you?"

"She didn't kill George. I did," Tom said from the floor. "I had to."

I thought about George lying on the floor behind the jewelry counter with the pearls tied around his neck. "You shot him but he didn't die. That's why you had to strangle him with the pearls."

"Poetic, don't you think?" Tom said. "I made every arrangement to get that necklace through customs, but George outsmarted me. When it ended up in his wife's store, I had to get it back."

"You killed George over this necklace?" I asked.

"That necklace was for me. My husband made a very big mistake when he cheated on me. For a million dollar necklace, I could forgive the affair."

I didn't know if Nick had gotten my message or not. The bullet Joyce had fired had bounced off of the ceiling but if she fired again, things might be different. There were twenty feet between us. If Joyce rushed me, I wouldn't get away.

My mind flashed over the emergency supplies in my pockets. Rope. Duct tape. Scissors.

Scissors.

I reached into my pocket and felt around for the scissors. "And Aguilar? Why kill him?"

Tom spoke. "If he'd told me where to find the necklace, he might still be alive."

"He was a criminal," Joyce added dismissively. "He deserved to die."

I looked back and forth between Tom and Joyce Kenner. Tom, who had killed two people, now bleeding on the floor of the camping store from a gunshot wound inflicted by his wife. Joyce, who showed no signs of distaste over her husband's actions. They were certifiable.

Joyce stepped forward and aimed the gun at me. "Now give me the pearls."

"Fine," I said. Before I could rethink my actions, I pulled the necklace out of my pocket and sliced through the silk cord on which it was strung. Individual knots between the pearls kept them from scattering around our feet like I'd wanted.

Both Joyce and Tom's eyes went wild and crazy. "No!" Joyce screamed. I gripped the necklace tightly in my left hand and sliced through the silk cord at randomly spaced intervals. I grabbed at the end of the silk cord and pushed against the lustrous black pearls. One by one they slid over the knots between them and fell, bouncing against the cold marble floor and scattering wildly. Joyce tossed the gun to the floor and dropped to her knees, clawing at the rapidly scattering orbs. Several rolled into the stream of blood that trickled out of the wound in Tom's thigh.

I grabbed the gun and aimed it at Joyce. I knew I couldn't pull the trigger.

"NIIIIIIIICK!!!" I yelled. "I need heeeeeeeeelp!"

The Lycra of Joyce's catsuit displayed a lean, muscular body that had been kept hidden under palazzo pants and caftans. This was no pudgy middle-aged wife. This was a woman who took great pains to fight the aging process with perky man-made breasts, sandblasted porcelain skin, pearly white teeth. But it would take a lot of high priced stylists to make Joyce Kenner regain the appearance of a society lady after this. Suddenly, the pile of lingerie made sense. She was a desperate wife somewhere past middle age, watching younger women get the attention she once received. She was down but not out.

Her hand shot out and caught me at my knees. I fell. She crawled over me and pressed a wool blanket into my face. "Why are you protecting her? She's a tramp. She's having my husband's baby. She's destroying my life!"

She pressed the blanket down over my nose. I couldn't breathe. I turned my head one way and then the other. She didn't let go. Her knees were on my arms and I couldn't move. Where was Nick? I closed my eyes and felt dizzy from the lack of oxygen.

And then the weight of her lifted and the blanket was pulled from my face. Nick dropped down beside me. I put my hand on my throat and gasped for breath. Joyce stood up and ran. Her foot caught on the pearls that were scattered on the floor and her feet shot out from under her.

Nick grabbed a bundle of black tree-climbing rope and wrapped it around Joyce. He knotted the ends and secured her to a fixture with D-Clamps.

"You heard me," I said between ragged breaths. "You were in the ceiling. I didn't think you'd come."

He put his hands on either side of my face. "Are you kidding? That's the first time you ever asked me for help." He pulled me into a hug. "I'm a firm believer in positive reinforcement."

Finally!

Before I knew it, sirens pierced the air. I unlocked the mall doors and watched a squadron of cop cars and an ambulance pull into the parking lot. Several cops and EMTs filtered out of their cars and charged into the building. Tom Kenner was moved to a gurney and rolled out. Joyce Kenner was handcuffed. Nick and I sat by the camping display, his arm around me, a blanket not dissimilar to the one I bought the night of our "overnight surveillance" wrapped around us.

And then a voice I hadn't heard for the past five months said, "Quit it with the cuddling and tell me what you're mixed up in this time."

In the two years that I'd been back in Ribbon, I never thought I'd be so happy to hear that voice. I looked up at dear, sweet, ornery, tan-from-Tahiti Detective Loncar.

Nick leaned close to my ear. "I hope you don't mind. I called for backup after the gunshots."

I smiled at Nick and then gave Loncar my most stern expression. "It's about time you came back from vacation," I said.

32

CHRISTMAS EVE

The night before Christmas, we gathered for a party at Cat's house. Cat had recovered from the past week. She was dressed in a vibrant purple dress and the pearl necklace that George had left behind in the fireplace. Her shiny red hair framed her face, and her smile, that had been in hiding for the past week, now reached her eyes. If all went as planned, her baby would arrive in a few weeks. The glow of pregnancy had eradicated any residual negativity from George's death.

Eddie adjusted the tinsel on Cat's Christmas tree. Dante sat on the sofa drinking eggnog. Nick was in the kitchen assembling us a plate of hors d'oeuvres. Other people mingled. Both Cat's and George's families had finally arrived thanks to a break in the weather. Neighbors who'd been stopping by all week with casseroles now enjoyed a glass of champagne. The vast array of sympathy flowers had been layered with colorful red poinsettias and lent a cheerful backdrop to the party.

I was dressed in the ivory fringed dress that I'd tried on the night we found George's body. The hardest part of the evening had been accessorizing, since the dress called for several long strands of pearls. In deference to what had gone down, I forwent the pearls and wore a band around my hair with a small flower on the side. My only other accessory was the engagement ring.

Christmas had come way too quickly this year. I'd been so preoccupied with Cat's situation that I'd barely noticed the dates changing on the calendar. My vacation had sped by in a blur of early mornings, late nights, crime scene clean-up, and suspicion. When Nick had tactfully pointed out that the holiday was in two days, I swore he made it up. It hadn't taken much more than a cross reference to the closest four desk calendars to prove him right. One, he could fake. Four sent me into a panic.

"Don't worry about it," he'd said. "The holidays are about being with friends and family, not about presents. I'll help you forget about what happened."

What happened.

Tom and Joyce Kenner had enjoyed a long marriage and a certain lifestyle thanks to his business. But Tom had risked that marriage on more than one occasion by having affairs on the side. Joyce pretended to look the other way as long as Tom made it up to her with jewelry, but this last time was too much. When she found out he had a dalliance with an employee from the mall, she threatened the kind of divorce that would leave him rubbing two pennies together trying to make a nickel.

So Tom did what he always did. He faked the paperwork on a valuable necklace to get it through customs. He canceled the order to the retailer, intending to declare the merchandise a loss and give it to Joyce instead. The value of the necklace was close to a million dollars, but to Tom it was worth the price of forgiveness.

But George, his newest sales rep, was eager to be successful. Unaware of the true value of the necklace, he convinced Cat to buy the canceled order for Catnip so his new employer would be out nothing.

Tom threatened George about the necklace. During his interrogation, Tom admitted to telling George to get that merchandise back or he'd never see his baby. He'd planned it all along: meet at Catnip after the holiday party, get the pearl necklace. But Shana burgled the store and I caught her in the act. Later, when the stolen pearls were discovered in Cat's office, Tom knew that somebody else was on to him. He could no longer expect the police to link the burglary to the murder. He tracked the thefts to Shana and Aguilar and committed a second murder, hoping Shana's confession would lead him to what he was really after. Aguilar would have made a better scapegoat, but one small detail kept Tom from killing Shana instead.

His affair had been with her.

Shana, unaware of the value of the missing necklace, had given Tom the only other necklace from Kenner & Winn left in the store: the one I'd put on hold. Tom used it to strangle Aguilar. If I had thought more about that and less about clothing karma, I might have realized Shana knew more than she'd admitted. The million dollar necklace that I'd destroyed inside the camping store had been dropped when Aguilar tried to hide the stolen jewelry in the ceiling of Cat's office.

George, not willing to risk the life of Cat or his unborn child, faked the fight with Cat and told her he needed space. I liked to believe that he planned all along to reconcile with Cat when things blew over. Nobody saw murder coming— especially people who lived on the right side of the law.

As for Joyce's rant when she attacked me? I had myself to blame. When I'd found her shopping for lingerie at Catnip and told her that Cat had gotten pregnant in April, it coincided with Tom's latest discretion. Cat moved from the "pregnant lesbian" column to the "scheming other woman" one. In Joyce's mind, destroying Cat's life was simply payback for an affair Cat had never had.

The doorbell rang, but Cat was caught behind a throng of family members and neighbors. She signaled to me to answer it. When I opened the door, Jim and Lela stood outside. I invited them in. Jim helped Lela out of her chinchilla coat and I looked away, remembering what she'd worn (or not) the last time she'd removed it. Tonight, she was tastefully dressed in a red wrap dress. Even under the jersey, or in spite of it, I could tell the woman had a great body. Maybe that's why she was comfortable parading around in her undies.

"I wouldn't mind seeing you in one of her outfits," a voice whispered in my ear.

"I don't see what's so special about a wrap dress," I countered.

"I was talking about her *other* outfits."

I turned around and faced Dante. "I don't think I own an outfit like those."

"Shame." Dante handed me a flute of champagne. As I held the glass to my lips, I watched him take notice of the engagement ring on my left hand. "So that's it," he said.

I shrugged. "That's it."

"He's a lucky guy," he said. He tapped his flute of champagne against mine and walked away.

I threaded my way through the crowd toward Nick. He stood by the tree, talking to Lela and Jim.

"What I don't understand is how you came to think I had something to do with the murders," Jim said.

It was Lela who answered him. "Honey, we have been acting a little suspicious. It wouldn't take much for someone to think we were up to something. Consider it from their point of view."

"And then we saw the pictures from my office," Cat said.

"What pictures?" Jim asked. "Oh, no. You installed a camera in your office? How much did you see?"

"Let's just say we saw a little more than a business meeting," Cat said tactfully.

Lela turned beet red and slapped Jim's arm playfully. "I told you it was icky," she said.

Jim put his arm around her. "From now on, only your place or mine. Until we agree on a house that can become ours." She turned her face away from him and he kissed her on the cheek.

"I'm sorry I suspected you," I said. "Someone was going after my friend and I couldn't let that happen."

Jim smiled. "Maybe someday you'll think of us as friends, too."

"Remember, Jim, Samantha is a very good customer," Cat said. "You might want to make sure 'someday' is sooner rather than later."

I looked at Cat. "What does that mean?"

"Didn't they tell you?" she said. She had a hand on her very pregnant belly. "I'm selling the store back to Jim and he and Lela are going to run it together. When we thought Lela was taking something from my office, that was Jim's offer. He was afraid it would get lost so she took it and gave it to him and he gave it to you."

"Are you okay with that?"

"That store was a part of my life for a while but it's time to move on to something new."

I leaned in close and whispered in her ear. "Full-time mom? Are you sure?"

"I'm sure," she said. "Now, come with me. I want you to open your present."

"You didn't have to get me a present."

"Oh yes, I did. I hope you don't think it's weird." She pointed to a flat box under the tree. I picked it up and shook it. The contents rattled. Cat giggled. I tore off the paper and opened the box. Inside was a suite of black pearl jewelry: earrings, bracelet, and necklaces. I slammed the box shut.

"Don't worry, they're knockoffs!" she said. "But they're perfect with that dress. I couldn't let you not accessorize because of me."

I added the jewelry to my outfit and hugged her. Nick put his arm around me. The party pulsed with a level of merriment and joy that we all needed.

The party broke up hours later when the snowstorm started up again. Nick popped his head into the room to see if I was ready to go. He held my coat in his hands.

"Go ahead," Cat said. "You've earned a Merry Christmas as much as anybody."

"Are you going to be okay? There's been a lot of change in your life in the past week. A week ago you said all men were rats."

"Isn't it wild how things turned out?" She put her hand on her throat and touched the pearls. "My husband didn't leave me. You're marrying Nick. And my brother is moving in to help when the baby comes."

"Wild" didn't begin to cover it.

Nick invited me to spend Christmas with him and his dad. After presents had been unwrapped and champagne had been drunk, he held out his hand. "I have one more present for you, but it's in my bedroom."

"Your dad is asleep in his recliner!"

"My dad knows about the present. He helped me get it ready."

Curiosity took over.

"Trust me," he said.

I followed him to his bedroom. A giant box, about six feet high and six feet wide, sat in the middle of the room wrapped in a mosaic of wrapping paper squares. A large tab dangled from the top of the box with lettering that read *PULL HERE*.

I pulled the tab and the box fell open like a drawbridge. Inside were stacks upon stacks of white boxes, all labeled with Nick's signature logo. There were too many to count, but I hadn't seen that many matching shoe boxes together since the day I'd stumbled upon Nick's delivery truck in New York City eleven years ago.

"You were my muse. My inspiration. This whole collection was about you. I wanted you to be the first person to have it. *That's* what kept me in Italy."

I'd like to say that Nick got something special too, but he didn't. He fell asleep long before I was done trying on shoes.

Discover the popular series that stars
Samantha Kidd, fashionable flatfoot in heels!

You'll love Samantha Kidd, former buyer turned amateur sleuth. Follow her through the fashion industry as she takes on bad guys in great style. This madcap series is the first from national bestselling author Diane Vallere.

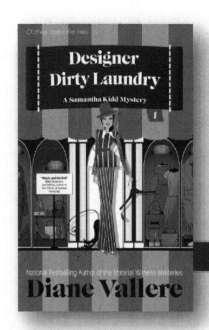

Designer
Dirty
Laundry

Samantha Kidd #1

Samantha Kidd, ex-buyer turned trend specialist, designed her future with couture precision, but finding the fashion director's corpse on day one leaves her hanging by a thread. When the killer fabricates evidence that puts the cops on her hemline, her new life begins to unravel. She trades high fashion for dirty laundry and reveals a cast of designers out for blood. Now this flatfoot in heels must keep pace with a diabolical designer before she gets marked down for murder.

Buyer, Beware

Samantha Kidd #2

Out-of-work fashion expert Samantha Kidd is strapped. But when the buyer of handbags for a hot new retailer turns up dead and Samantha is recruited for the job, the opportunity comes with a caveat: she's expected to find some answers. The police name a suspect but the label doesn't fit. Samantha turns to a sexy stranger for help but as the walls close around her like a snug satin lining, she must get a handle on the suspects, or risk being caught in the killer's clutches.

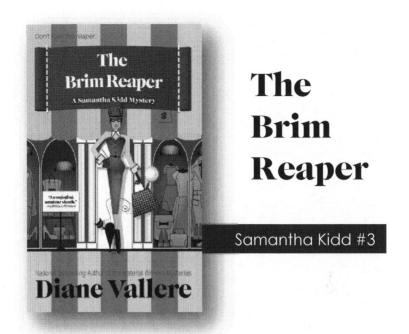

The Brim Reaper

Samantha Kidd #3

Diane Vallere

When an over-the-top collection of vintage Hollywood costumes comes to Samantha Kidd's hometown, it brings a hat box full of hype. Close friend Eddie is in charge of the exhibit but when hype turns to homicide, he turns to Samantha for help. Brimming with good intentions, she loops in the cops, but after one too many cloche calls, she's soon in over her head. If she can tear the lid off the investigation, it might mean a feather in her fedora. And if she can't? She might get capped.

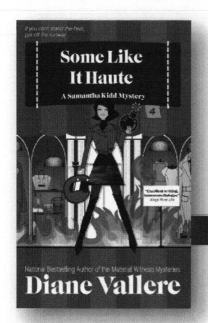

Some Like It Haute

Samantha Kidd #4

Fashion expert Samantha Kidd is in the hot seat. After agreeing to help her ex-boyfriend's former girlfriend with a runway show, she's attacked in the parking lot outside, landing in the hospital. And when a garment goes up in flames on the catwalk the day after the attack, the situation turns explosive. She recruits a smokin' hot photographer to turn up the heat on the investigation, but even the third degree won't expose an angry arsonist. With a crash course in sizzle, Samantha's curiosity leads her into another inferno, and this time she either faces the fire or gets burned.

Grand Theft Retro

Samantha Kidd #5

When Samantha Kidd's job at Retrofit Magazine leads her into the archives of seventies style, she's prepared to report on patchwork velvet and platform shoes, but she never expected to uncover the theft of a major collection of samples from runway shows that took place before disco died. And when the guilty party threatens Samantha's family and friends, her priority shift into protection mode. The investigation heats up faster than fondue over sterno, and all too soon Samantha learns that while beat goes on, there's no guarantee that she'll go on with it.

ABOUT THE AUTHOR

After close to two decades working for a top luxury retailer, Diane Vallere traded fashion accessories for accessories to murder. Diane started her own detective agency at age ten and has maintained a passion for shoes, clues, and clothes ever since. Sign up for her newsletter for contests, free stories, and more at www.dianevallere.com.

Made in the USA
Middletown, DE
29 January 2017